Praise for Claire Thompson's *Our Man Friday*

"Our Man Friday is a wonderful love story... Ms. Thompson has long been one of my favorite authors and Our Man Friday fit in with her other terrific books!"

~ *Just Erotic Romance Reviews*

Rating: 5 Angels "...Our Man Friday is just one example of Ms. Thompson's fantastic writing style. She doesn't just hand you a story with erotic scenes that require ice and a fan but delivers real human situations for personable characters."

~ *Fallen Angel Reviews*

"...The characters become attached to each other neither too quickly nor too slowly. The pace felt realistic and not at all dragged-out, with each character coming to terms with his or her feelings in a way that made sense for that particular character....this was an excellent story, well-written and well-thought-out. I highly enjoyed it and I'll definitely be recommending it to others who are fans of ménage a trois romance stories."

~ *Rainbow Review*

Look for these titles by
Claire Thompson

Now Available:

Handyman

Our Man Friday

Polar Reaction

Our Man Friday

Claire Thompson

A SAMHAIN PUBLISHING, LTD. publication.

Samhain Publishing, Ltd.
577 Mulberry Street, Suite 1520
Macon, GA 31201
www.samhainpublishing.com

Our Man Friday
Copyright © 2009 by Claire Thompson
Print ISBN: 978-1-60504-446-0
Digital ISBN: 978-1-60504-377-7

Editing by Sasha Knight
Cover by Natalie Winters

First Samhain Publishing, Ltd. electronic publication: December 2008
First Samhain Publishing, Ltd. print publication: October 2009

Dedication

To Sasha Knight, who has helped me to become a better writer with constant dedication, patience and humor.

Chapter One

All eyes in the room were on him as he walked toward the bar. Tall, with dark hair curling down the back of his neck, broad shouldered and gorgeous, he was the object of everyone's attention. The men were either scowling or drooling, depending on their sexual orientation, the women staring with unabashed lust on their faces.

He only had eyes for Cassidy. She stood as he approached her, gasping as he reached for her, taking her without question or permission into his strong arms. His grip was rough as he pulled her close. His cock was like steel pressed against her stomach. Her nipples hardened, her pussy instantly aching for him.

He didn't kiss her so much as claim her mouth, his tongue and lips sliding against hers while his hands roamed her body as if he owned it. She couldn't have escaped him, even if she'd wanted to. The room was strangely silent, except for the rasping of her breath and the beating of her heart. He stopped his kiss only long enough to whisper in her ear, "You belong to me. I'll never let you go..."

Cassidy realized she was staring at the handsome stranger, her fantasies getting the better of her. Embarrassed, she swiveled back toward the bar. Someone slid onto the stool beside her. The heat rose in her cheeks. She let her hair fall forward to hide her face.

The bartender ambled over. "What can I do ya for?"

"I'll have an Innis and Gunn, if you've got it." The accent wasn't quite British but every bit as appealing. Was it Irish? It seemed softer somehow, rolling and lilting over his tongue. She wanted to hear it again.

"Sorry. Never heard of it."

"How about a Raven Ale?"

"Nope."

"Dark Island?" A pause. "Dragonhead Stout? Arran Blonde?"

Cassidy stole a sidelong glance at the man. She looked away, her breath catching in her throat. He was even better looking close up.

"No Scottish ale at this worthy establishment, I take it? Ah well. What have you got on tap?"

"Coors, Lone Star and Bud Light. You want that fancy stuff, you're in the wrong place," Ted, the bartender, growled, disapproval ripe in his tone.

The stranger either didn't notice or didn't care. "Make it a Coors, my friend. And another of whatever this lovely lady's drinking."

Startled but pleased, Cassidy shook back her hair and turned her smile toward the stranger. She felt a surge of heat as their eyes met, and a catch and then quickening of her breath.

He was wearing a black T-shirt that hugged round, strong biceps and a broad, shapely chest. His jeans were faded nearly to white, a hole in the left knee. He wore a thin silver chain around his neck. He placed a guitar case, backpack and much-used duffel bag on the floor beside his stool.

He was looking directly at her, his smile slow and easy, a kind of challenge in his eyes. She could feel the man's energy emanating from him, as if he were sending out electric signals to her nipples, the current arcing through her body, rapidly finding its way to her sex.

Her eyes were drawn to the not-insubstantial bulge in his jeans. She forced herself to look up and saw he was staring straight at her with large clear gray eyes that crinkled at the corners as he bestowed a heart-stopping smile on her. The contrast of the light eyes against tan skin and black hair was arresting. She wasn't sure if it was a trick of the light or what, but his eyes were nearly silver, their gaze captivating.

In a rich brogue, he offered, "I never could resist a ginger-haired lass."

Cassidy's hair, which had been carrot-orange when she was a child, had mercifully eased itself into more of a reddish auburn as she'd matured. There was still too much of it, curling and springing around her face, refusing to stay tucked behind her ears, escaping in tendrils from any effort to tie or pin it back. Though she had a kind of love-hate relationship with her hair, she found herself thoroughly charmed by his compliment. "Thanks."

Ted returned with two mugs of beer. The stranger lifted his toward Cassidy. "To your health." He took a long drink. Cassidy knew she was staring but couldn't seem to pull her eyes away from him. He set down the glass, his lips wet with foam. She experienced a strange urge to rub her thumb across his lower lip and then follow it with her tongue.

She pulled up his T-shirt to feel his hard, smooth chest. Oblivious of the onlookers, she bent over him, biting his nipples playfully as her hands sought and found his zipper. Unabashedly, she climbed over his lap, pushing him back against the empty stool beside him. Lifting her dress, she straddled his cock, pushing away the flimsy satin of her panties so she could mount him then and there...

She realized he was watching her, his eyes narrowed, as if privy to the steamy daydream that was making her panties moist. Cassidy swallowed and blinked. Her mouth was open and she snapped it shut. She lifted her own mug to hide her blazing cheeks.

"Forgive my lack of manners." He inclined his head toward her, a half smile on his face. "Kye McClellan, at your service."

"Cassidy. Cassidy Luke."

Kye leaned down, picking up the battered olive-green backpack and duffel bag in one hand, the guitar case in the other. For one terrible second she thought he was leaving. She almost blurted, *Wait, don't go!* Thankfully, she held her tongue long enough for him to add, "Would you care to join me in a booth?"

It didn't even occur to Cassidy to say no. She followed him to an empty booth, settling across from him on the cool, black leather seat. For the first time in three years, someone was edging Ian Tanner out of that secret place in her heart, or at least trying to insert himself alongside him.

"So, you're a musician? Are you with a band? Are you on tour from Scotland?"

"I just carry the guitar around to impress girls." His eyes twinkled and he laughed an infectious laugh. Cassidy laughed too. "Actually I do play, but not professionally."

Cassidy nodded. The guy didn't need any props to impress the girls, that was for sure.

"Actually," he continued with that delightful Scottish lilt, "I came to the States with...a friend. Things didn't work out, alas, so here I find myself, with all my worldly possessions, footloose and fancy-free, as they say." A shadow of pain washed over his face, gone as quickly as it had come.

She'd touched on a nerve. What woman in her right mind would let a guy like him go? Of course, as Cassidy well knew, logic didn't always play a part when it came to matters of the heart.

Apparently ready to change the subject, Kye added, "If I

may be so bold, what's a lovely woman like yourself doing alone in a bar on a Friday evening?"

The troubles with the business, which she'd actually completely forgotten since laying eyes on the handsome Scot, returned in full force. She sighed. "I just needed to get away, I guess. I needed to think."

"What about? Or is it too personal?"

"It's my business." She gave a rueful laugh. "Everything's going great, except that I'm afraid I'm running it into the ground and I'm too scared to tell my partner."

Kye nodded sympathetically. Cassidy hadn't told anyone of her fears for their jewelry business, least of all Ian. It had taken all her powers of persuasion to get him to make the leap ten months before, leaving his safe but dull, dead-end job as a jewelry repairman for a chain of mall store locations. Though both only twenty-six, Cassidy had managed to convince him to follow his dream of creating his own line of jewelry.

She'd readily quit her job taking portraits for Walmart, though she continued to freelance for weddings and bar mitzvahs and the occasional commissioned portrait. But mostly she'd thrown herself into getting Ian Tanner Designs off the ground.

Their startup capital for materials and tools had consisted of their combined liquidated retirement funds, which totaled a pitiful five thousand three hundred dollars between them, after taxes and penalties for early withdrawal.

Because Ian was the creative force behind the company, they had agreed Cassidy would handle the production, marketing and finance of their fledgling enterprise. She enjoyed the production and marketing aspects, lovingly photographing the pieces to show them at their best advantage, and writing concise, attractive descriptions to titillate the online buyers on their new website, which she'd designed.

She liked going around to the local jewelry stores, watching the owners' eyes widen with appreciation when they saw what beautiful pieces she had to sell. Really, Ian's jewelry sold itself.

Cassidy knew she was flying by the seat of her pants, but so far she'd managed to pull it off. Her lack of business savvy hadn't been a problem, or at least not a big one, until recently. But with orders starting to come in from their online site, plus reorders from local vendors, they'd had to start acting more like a real business.

If Cassidy was bad with money, Ian was even worse. He had no idea what anything cost, from a pound of hamburger to the gems and fine metals he needed to create his works of art. He just knew what he liked. It was touching in a way—he would ask Cassidy if they could afford whatever it was he wanted for his latest creation, and trusted her completely with all the financial decisions.

Cassidy had come to the bar to forget her troubles, at least for a while. She hadn't planned on sharing them with a stranger, especially not one so hot she'd scorch her fingers if she touched him. Yet something in his face made her want to confide in him. To ask him what to do. It was tempting to use this guy as a sounding board, if nothing else. He seemed genuinely eager to listen. Even if he had no insight to offer, she'd still get to look at his handsome face while she talked. After all, it wasn't as if she were giving away state secrets.

Kye was watching her, his expression open and kind. She decided to follow her instincts. First she gave him the thumbnail sketch of how the venture got started. He listened intently, asking questions along the way and expressing great enthusiasm, which gratified her.

"It sounds terrific, Cassidy. To be making money in the first year of any new venture is in itself an accomplishment."

"Things *should* be terrific, but they're not. I'm in trouble. It's cash flow. We haven't got any. The stupid thing is, Ian can't make stuff fast enough for me to sell it. And we're getting top dollar. Some of the more upscale boutiques are starting to take notice. Everything looks great—on paper." She sighed, dropping her head into her hands.

"Tell me," Kye urged. "Sometimes just to talk through our troubles gives us a new perspective."

Cassidy nodded but sighed again. "Talking it through isn't going to help me, I'm afraid. Unfortunately, neither of us has a head for business. I thought I could make it work, just through sheer determination, but I get so caught up in what I'm doing, I forget about the boring details. I'm so damn busy, what with the site, the catalog, the sales to local vendors—it's amazing I even remember to buy toilet paper."

"Sounds like you need someone to help out with the more mundane aspects of running a business. Someone with experience with that sort of thing. That would free you up to focus on what you really love. Businesses thrive when the right people are doing what they're good at. You can't shove a square peg into a round hole."

"We couldn't possibly afford to hire anyone at this point. I don't want to tell Ian how bad it is. He's having the time of his life."

"Forgive me for prying, but is Ian your, uh, boyfriend?"

Cassidy felt her face heat and hoped it didn't show as a blush. She shrugged. "No, we're just business partners. Well," she amended, "and we bought a house together. We live together."

"As roommates..."

"Yeah." The warmth slid down her neck.

Kye eyed her dubiously, but left it at that, for which she was grateful. "So tell me more about the business. Business, from the sound of things, is booming, but you run out of cash before the end of the cycle. What's going wrong, do you think?"

Cassidy answered honestly. "I wish I knew." She flushed. "I forgot to pay a credit card last month. I mean, it just slipped my mind. Well, they cancelled the card! They called to let me know it had been sent to collection. I couldn't tell Ian."

"They cancelled after just one missed payment?" Kye cocked a skeptical eyebrow.

"Well, maybe two. I have so much to handle, you have no idea." She knew she sounded defensive. "The frustrating thing is we have the demand. I just can't seem to get any cash. We had a COD delivery arrive yesterday, important gems Ian needs to finish a big order, and I didn't have the damn money. I had to refuse the package. All these boutiques want to buy the jewelry, but they want terms. Basically they want the stuff free for thirty to ninety days. So I have all these accounts receivable but meanwhile I can't cover basic bills."

"Very common for startups." He stroked his chin. Cassidy couldn't help but admire his firm, square jaw. "I could help you, I think."

"What do you mean? How?"

"I have quite a bit of experience in this sort of thing. I have an accounting background. I helped run my family's business for a few years before I took to world travel to seek fame and fortune." He grinned, his eyes sparkling.

"Oh, I couldn't ask—"

"From the sound of it, you've got a great little company with enormous potential." Cassidy couldn't help but glow at this remark. "But on the path you're on now, you'll be out of business by the end of the year." The glow rapidly faded.

"What you need are some basic procedures to ensure you don't run out of cash in the middle of your business cycle. You need to organize and determine your expenses. You need a budget and a business plan, especially now that you're growing rapidly. And most importantly, you need a line of credit, a revolving line of credit with a bank, so you can draw on the cash when you need it, and repay it when the funds come in."

"Who would lend us—?"

"With a sound business plan, plus an income statement and balance sheet to show your inventory and accounts receivable, you'll easily qualify for a small line. You borrow on it regularly, and pay it back like clockwork. You establish yourself as a reliable company. As the business grows, they'll want to stay involved. It's what banks do. It's how they make their money."

"I wouldn't have the first idea about a business plan or balance sheets. I can barely balance a checkbook."

"You're in luck." He laughed but continued in a serious vein. "I'd be quite willing to take a look at your books, such as they are, and see if we can't make some sense of it all."

Cassidy was taken aback. Offering advice was one thing— looking at the books quite another. Maybe in Scotland people just offered to involve themselves in a stranger's personal finances, but Cassidy wasn't at all sure she was comfortable with the idea. Especially because the business belonged to Ian as well.

"Thanks just the same, but I wouldn't think of asking—"

"Forgive me. I've overstepped, I can see that." Kye put his hand on her arm, his smile disarming her. "I only offer because I do have some experience in the area and well..." He hesitated and Cassidy could see he was uncomfortable.

He looked down at the table as if marshaling his thoughts. "The thing is, I'm in a bit of a bind myself. I was hoping to barter my services."

Cassidy's curiosity was piqued. "What did you want to barter?" She licked her lower lip, unable to control the thought of offering him her body in exchange for his business acumen. Offering to climb over those thick, strong thighs and straddle his hard cock, riding him until she screamed with pleasure...

Seeing the gleam in his eye, she had the sudden uneasy feeling he was peeking into her dirty mind. She lifted her beer mug to her face.

Kye spread his hands on the table and looked down at them. When he spoke, his voice was subdued. "As I mentioned, I came to Houston with someone I met back in Europe. We kind of had a thing going for a while, but it just wasn't working out. It was time for me to go." He spoke lightly, but the smile on his lips didn't rise to his eyes. Cassidy saw the pain flicker in them and again wondered what kind of stupid woman would let a guy like him go.

He continued. "We agreed this morning it was better if we parted company. I have the wee problem of a place to stay for the next few days." He patted his guitar case and added, "There's an audition in Austin coming up at the end of the week with a decent band looking for a lead guitar. I was thinking about catching a bus up there, but I need somewhere to crash till then. I would be happy to assist in whatever way possible with the business while I'm here, if the arrangement interests you."

Oh, it interests me, all right. She knew she was focused more on his bulging biceps and heart-tugging smile than his potential skills as a business consultant and silently admonished herself to get a grip. "What if you don't get the gig?"

Kye waved his hand and shrugged. "I'm not worried. Something will come up. I always land on my feet." With his confident, easygoing air, his devastatingly good looks and his natural charm, Cassidy could well believe it.

He went on, "In exchange for a temporary bed, I'd be more than willing to have a look at your business records and help you organize and prepare for a bank visit. I'm also quite handy in the kitchen and don't mind having a go with a broom and dustpan."

18

Was this guy for real? Was this a genuine offer of service in exchange for room and board, or was he just looking for a way to get into her home, possibly to rob them blind? He knew she had a man at home, so she doubted he intended to try and have his way with her, though the idea wasn't entirely without appeal.

Shit, even if he was just looking for a place to crash and didn't know a debit from a credit (which Cassidy herself did not), who could turn away such a handsome, sexy guy? Who would want to?

It wasn't like they didn't have the space. They lived and worked out of the shabby but comfortable Victorian they'd snagged for a fantastic price for Houston's trendy Neartown. And if he wanted to cook, all the better. Cassidy wasn't sure if the ancient oven that had come with the house even worked, but if he wanted to find out, it was okay by her.

She looked up at Kye, who was waiting patiently for her decree. She lost her train of thought as she stared into his eyes. He sat back, folding his thickly muscled arms over his broad chest. There was a kindness in his face, an openness that appealed to her even more than his sexy bod.

Her gut told her he was on the level. "Let me just call my partner."

Kye went to the bar to get another beer and, she figured, to give her privacy during the call. The house phone went to voice mail so she tried Ian's cell. This too went to voice mail. She smiled to herself. He was probably so busy creating he didn't even notice it.

When the phone beeped, she left a message. "Hi, Ian. It's me. Listen, I met this guy at Jim's Place. Turns out he's a business wizard. He's from Scotland and he needs a place to stay for a day or two. He has some really great ideas for the business. I thought I'd bring him home to meet you. Okay? See you soon."

19

Kye returned, sliding back into the booth with two beer mugs. "Everything okay?"

"I didn't reach him, but, yeah, it's okay. I left a message."

Kye leaned forward, putting his hand over hers. Cassidy squelched any lingering trepidation as he warmed her with his smile. "Thank you, Cassidy. I really appreciate it."

She looked down at his large hand covering her much smaller one. His fingers were long, the tips blunt, the nails square and clean. Her arm tingled as she imagined him sliding those fingers along her skin, moving upward toward her shoulder. Her nipples were erect and probably showing through the thin material of her lacey bra and tank top. She pulled her hand from beneath his and crossed her arms over her chest.

She thought suddenly about the condition of the house, about the disarray in the huge living room they'd commandeered for Ian's studio and her work area. They were both so focused on getting the business up and running, neither had the time nor the inclination to do much housekeeping. The kitchen had a sink full of dishes and a floor that hadn't been washed in weeks. Despite their best intentions, though most of the boxes were unpacked, pictures had yet to be hung and there were no curtains on the windows.

Oh well. There were worse things than a messy house. Somehow she didn't think Kye would mind too much. The spare bedroom was clean. It just needed sheets on the bed.

Though she hadn't intended to pry, she found herself saying, "So it was an amiable split? No broken hearts?"

Kye shrugged. "Maybe cracked a bit. In retrospect, I guess it was just one of those flings—you know, you connect with people when you're traveling in a more immediate way than you would otherwise. Sometimes when people return to their home turf, they realize they were just kidding themselves. They return to 'the real world', I guess you'd say. I apparently was not part of that real world."

He looked so sad she wanted to lean over and hold him. Why were things always such a mess when it came to relationships? Inwardly she sighed, thinking of her own confusion and longing when it came to love. Aloud she said, "Was she American?"

"Actually it wasn't a she," Kye answered, his cheeks dimpling. "It was a guy."

Chapter Two

Gay? Had she misread his cues, comments and body language so completely? Cassidy's stunned reaction must have shown on her face. "Not what you were expecting to hear, I'm guessing?"

"No, it's not that, I mean, well, yes." Cassidy struggled to recover. "I usually have a pretty good read on that sort of thing."

Kye again put his hand over hers, his touch warm and firm. "Your read was quite accurate. It just so happens I'm attracted to men as well. That's not so unusual, is it? You give me the impression of someone who's open-minded about such things."

"Yeah. I'm totally cool with it." In fact she wasn't sure what she was with it, at least in regard to him. What was her problem? Had she already planned to seduce the guy, when on the surface they had only bartered business advice for a bed?

Yeah, she admitted, she had. She could almost feel his hard, strong body covering hers, her nipples mashed beneath his chest, her sex soaked with desire as he eased himself into her heat...

Kye shook her out of her mini-fantasy. "Would you like another beer?"

Forcing the fantasy from her mind, Cassidy glanced at her watch. It was already after eight. "I hadn't realized it was so late. Say, have you had dinner yet?" When he shook his head no, she continued. "I was going to stop and pick up some tamales. Then I could take you home and introduce you to Ian."

"Sounds like a plan, though I have no idea what tamales are."

Cassidy grinned. "Then you're in for a treat. Do you want to follow me?"

"I'd have to run awfully fast, I'm afraid. I have no car."

"No car in Houston? How do you get around?"

"I've only been here a few weeks. Until today I didn't need one."

Cassidy sensed the subject was a sore one. "No problem. You can come with me."

As they left the bar, Cassidy could feel the eyes of some of the regulars on her. She waved toward some gay friends of hers, George and Paul, who waved back. George, who was always telling her what a great catch Ian was and how foolish she was not to ensnare him, lifted a thumb approvingly into the air. She fervently hoped Kye hadn't seen the gesture.

Kye put his few possessions in the back of Cassidy's car and climbed into the passenger seat beside her as she started the engine. She pulled out of the parking lot, wondering what the hell had gotten into her. Picking up a stranger, taking him in her car, bringing him home to Ian? Was she certifiably insane? Yet she didn't feel panicked, nor did she really question the decision, though admittedly it wasn't like her to bring someone she'd just met home. Instinctively she knew she could trust this man. There was something about him that put her at ease, once she got past his devastatingly good looks.

They picked up tamales, enchiladas and refritos, and a six-pack of beer to go with it, before heading home. Kye insisted on paying.

Cassidy pulled into the driveway of the old house, with its

sagging wrap-around porch and small yard, the grass of which was in desperate need of cutting, bright yellow dandelions peeking here and there through the green. She was embarrassed at the place's bedraggled appearance.

She turned to offer her excuses, but Kye beat her to it. "What a *fantastic* old house. I love all the turrets and towers. This must be one of the older houses in Houston. This is really yours?"

The admiration was evident in his voice, and Cassidy's embarrassment was replaced, or at least mitigated, by pride. "Yeah. Well, the mortgage is ours." She flashed a rueful grin. "It was a foreclosure and we got it for an incredible deal. It's still a hefty monthly payment though. Sometimes I think we rushed into it."

"This house will return its investment tenfold, you can count on it. You made the right decision. It's a sound old place, I'm willing to bet. A few nails and a bit of paint will smarten it up nicely. Have you got a lawn mower?"

"Yes, though I guess you wouldn't know it from the looks of the lawn. That's Ian's job but he's been so busy..."

"That I can well understand. Perhaps in the morning I can give the yard a quick mow. I wouldn't mind a bit. I like to be occupied."

"Oh, I couldn't ask you—"

"And nor did you. I offered."

They climbed out of the car and walked to the front door. She opened the door, calling, "Hi, Ian. I'm back. I brought Mexican food and a new friend. Come out and meet him." She held her breath, waiting for Ian to appear. What was she nervous about? Kye wasn't her date, and anyway she didn't need Ian's permission to bring someone home.

After a moment Ian came into the large front hall, running his hands through his short blond hair so that it stood on end, making him look like he'd just woken up. It was a habit he had when he had been concentrating on something for a long time and was trying to return to the world, as he termed it. She had always found the gesture endearing, and her heart lurched at the sight of him.

"Ian. This is Kye McClellan. He's visiting from Scotland."

A flicker of a scowl crossed Ian's face though it was quickly replaced by a pleasant smile. They moved toward one another and shook hands. She knew Ian was wondering if the term *friend* was code for lover.

Ian and she were just friends—at least that's what she told anyone who asked. Only Jane, her sister, knew of her secret, desperate longing for more.

Ian and she had met three years before at the pool party of a mutual friend. Ian had been there with someone, a slim, blonde woman named Angela, who for much of the party had hung onto his arm as if someone had glued her there.

Somehow he had eventually disentangled himself from his date, approaching Cassidy as she was taking pictures of the mosaic tiles set into the concrete around the perimeter of the swimming pool. Cassidy was never without one of her cameras, and she liked to take pictures of things other people might find odd—a closeup of blades of grass when the sun hit them just so, or a child's chubby feet, shod in bright red plastic sandals.

After the initial small talk, they'd discussed color and design, and Ian had told her of his dream of creating his own line of jewelry, though back then that's all it had been—a dream. Aware of Ian's girlfriend splashing in the pool nearby, her eyes swiveling possessively toward him, their banter had been light and superficial, though there had been an undeniable attraction eddying and flowing just below the surface, at least on Cassidy's side.

Ian had asked for her email address, ostensibly to take her

up on her offer to photograph some of the pieces he'd been working on. They'd exchanged several long emails, veering from arranging a time and place to do the shoot all the way to what they each wanted out of life.

"There's something about him," Cassidy had confided to Jane. "Something different. He's thoughtful. He's got a poetic turn of mind. You should check out his MySpace page. His jewelry is really beautiful."

"Who are you kidding?" Jane, who had also been at the pool party, had teased. "You love the way his back muscles ripple when he dives into the pool. You love his streaky blond hair and his cute butt."

"Jane, shut *up*," Cassidy protested. "Not everything is about sex. He has a girlfriend anyway. Besides, we're on the same wavelength. Neither of us ever wants to get married. He agrees with me that relationships are vastly overrated."

"What would you know about relationships? Mom's right— you're too much the gypsy when it comes to love."

Cassidy was the first to admit this. In her twenty-six years she'd only been able to get to a certain level of intimacy with a guy before something in her DNA made her bolt. She just wasn't cut out to be with one guy, at least not for the long term. After a while she began to feel hemmed in. What would start out as easy and fun invariably slid into a fight for control, a battle of wills, or worse, plain old boredom.

Sex just seemed to complicate the matter, and Ian had been no exception. At first things had gone great between them. The fact he was involved with Angela had actually worked in their favor. It freed them both up just to be themselves. Neither was trying to impress the other as a potential lover. It was great to have a guy friend who was just a friend. And he was so easy to talk to. If she fantasized about him late at night, it was nobody's business but her own.

He, too, often said how great it was to have a friend who was a girl, but not a girlfriend. He liked being with a woman who didn't require constant reassurance about her appearance and sex appeal. He didn't have to walk on eggshells, worried that a casual remark would be taken the wrong way and lead to a night of sulking, which apparently was par for the course with Angela. It was obvious to Cassidy that he wasn't especially happy with Angela, but she was too smart to go there, not unless he brought it up first.

After she'd photographed his pieces, they'd gone out for a beer. He hadn't tried to hit on her. In fact, he'd spent a large part of the evening talking about Angela, and about his one serious relationship before that, the one that had soured him to the whole idea of getting too involved.

One day about a month into their friendship, Cassidy stopped by the jewelry shop where Ian worked just as he was finishing his shift. "Hey, Ian. I'm bored. Want to catch a movie or something?" Noticing his woebegone look, she added, "What's the matter? Did Angela leave you or something?"

She'd only been kidding, but Ian didn't smile. "Yeah," he answered, stunning her. He hadn't mentioned that anything was amiss between them, other than the usual bickering.

"Oh, Ian. I'm sorry. What happened?"

"Let's go get a beer, want to? I don't want to talk about it here."

"Sure, absolutely."

They went to Jim's Place, even then a favorite of Ian's, because it was quiet and close to Ian's Montrose apartment. Over a pitcher of beer, he told her what had happened. "I feel like such a jerk. I wasn't even in love with her, but walking in on her and my friend Kevin was like getting punched in the stomach. I was just so not expecting it."

"Who would expect that?" Cassidy commiserated. "What a

crummy thing to do."

"Yeah. In my apartment, no less. I mean, if you're going to fuck around on someone, at least have the grace to do it in your own place." He shook his head.

They finished the pitcher, and Ian, who held his liquor better than Cassidy, insisted on driving her to her apartment—they would pick up her car the next day. She invited him in, not consciously intending to seduce him, though in retrospect she realized the idea had begun to form the moment she found out he and Angela were history.

He joined her on the sofa, accepting a cup of coffee to sober up before he left. They talked some about relationships—how they never seemed to work out, at least not for either of them. Then, just like in a movie, Ian put his cup down, his golden brown eyes burning with a secret fire as he leaned toward her. She closed her eyes, her lips tingling in anticipation of his kiss.

There was no awkward fumbling, no hesitation, no newness to get past. He took her into his arms and kissed her until her heart was pounding high in her throat, her pussy throbbing and swollen with desire.

He stood, leaning down to scoop her into his arms. He carried her to her bedroom and laid her on the bed. She had never wanted someone as much as she'd wanted him. She didn't resist when he pulled her shirt over her head, unhooked her bra, slid down her pants and panties until she lay naked on the bed before him.

"Cassidy," he whispered, his voice urgent with longing.

Quickly he stripped. She stared at his strong, firm body, her eyes drawn to his long, thick cock, fully erect and pointing toward her. Leaning over her, he kissed her lips. He ran his tongue along her throat and collarbone to her nipple, and lower, leaving a trail of desire along her skin.

With gentle insistence he spread her legs, his tongue

seeking and finding her center. All the pent-up desire, hidden beneath her own staunch claim to herself that they were just friends, came boiling over. Teetering on the edge of orgasm, she was trembling when he finally entered her. Almost at once she began to climax, coming so hard and so long she passed out, only to awaken a few seconds later, wrapped in his strong arms.

That's when everything had changed.

The sex had remained fabulous, but everything else seemed to fall apart. Ian began to treat her differently. At first she just thought it was the newness of their being lovers. But instead of things getting better, they got worse. Gone was the easy banter. Somehow they had become stiff and uncertain around each other.

She realized she was treating him differently too. Instead of calling him just to talk about nothing or anything, she found herself weighing her words, afraid she might seem too needy or demanding, now that they were lovers. She missed the easiness of being around him. She missed being his friend, but she didn't know how to get back what they'd had.

About a month into Ian and Cassidy's new relationship as lovers, Angela solved the problem for them, in a roundabout way. At one in the morning, she showed up in tears at Ian's apartment. Her lip was cut, her right eye swollen shut. Kevin and she had been fighting and he'd gotten physical. She fell into Ian's arms, sobbing that she missed him and she was so sorry she'd fooled around on him.

Ian had settled her in his bed, after giving her a stiff brandy and some ibuprofen. Afterwards he'd called Cassidy, explaining what had happened. She was less than thrilled at the thought of Angela lying asleep in Ian's bed, but he clearly needed to talk things through. They agreed Angela should press charges against the bastard. As they talked about the situation, Cassidy lay back in her bed, feeling the comfortable, sweet ease they'd used to share slip back into their conversation.

Cassidy sighed. "I miss this."

"Yeah, me too. I don't know what happened exactly. Why we lost it." But they both knew.

"Maybe we're better as friends than lovers." Cassidy squeezed her eyes shut, mentally cursing herself. What was she saying?

She wasn't entirely sure how she'd expected Ian to react. Had she wanted him to stoutly deny it—to explode with outraged indignation, to swear his undying love, no matter the cost? Well, he hadn't.

There was a long pause, during which she wondered if he was still there. "Yeah. I guess you're right." Beneath the sadness in his tone, there was a finality that cut a fissure along her heart.

Angela chose that moment to call for him. Cassidy could hear her whine in the background.

"I have to go." The sadness gone, Ian's tone was crisp. "I'll call you in the morning and we'll figure this out."

He had called, but they hadn't figured it out. At least Cassidy hadn't. Angela had stayed with Ian for several more days, claiming to be afraid of Kevin returning to her place. Ian tried, unsuccessfully, to get her to press charges. Eventually he sent her away, but by then the change in the relationship between Cassidy and Ian had been wrought.

And truth to tell, it was easier being friends. Ian relaxed again and slowly things returned to the way they had been before. They began to talk seriously about starting the jewelry business, though it would be a while before they took the plunge.

She never forgot the touch of his lips against hers, or his hard, perfect cock sending spirals of buttery pleasure through her, but she cherished their friendship more. Over the years, she'd watched Ian date and then break up with woman after woman. She, too, had her share of casual relationships. None of them could hold a candle to Ian, in bed or out.

Maybe, as she often told her sister Jane, she just wasn't cut out for love.

Now she watched Ian and Kye sizing one another up, in that way males do, silently determining who was the alpha. If Cassidy had to pick, she'd have to say it was a tie. Breaking the silence, she offered, "Kye and I met at Jim's Place. I was telling him about the business. He has some good ideas that might help with cash flow."

Kye nodded enthusiastically. "It sounds like a terrific venture. I'd love to see some of your pieces. I'm fascinated with the creative mind."

Cassidy smiled. He'd said exactly the right thing. She interjected, "I'll just put out the food. We went to Maria's. Show him those pendants you're working on." Pride welled in her voice as she turned to Kye. "He can't make them fast enough. I have three shops on a waiting list. Wait'll you see how cool they are."

It was their most popular piece, a circle of yellow or white gold, with blue topaz, amethyst, citrine, peridot and garnets set in a beautiful pattern inside it. Ian always varied the design, making each an original.

Kye followed Ian into the studio while Cassidy veered off toward the dining room. She could hear the low rumble of masculine voices and was relieved their introduction had gone so smoothly.

A few minutes later the men joined her. Over dinner, Kye told them stories of his travels across the world. He was funny and relaxed, and had them both laughing over tales of his failure to communicate in various countries and the resulting snafus.

The beers drunk, they opened a bottle of Cabernet to go

with the plate of sopapillas stuffed with baked apples and cinnamon and sprinkled with brown sugar. They stayed at the table talking and laughing until the wine was gone and not even a crumb of the tasty dessert remained. At about eleven Ian excused himself to finish the piece he was working on.

Cassidy took Kye to the spare bedroom. She brought in sheets from the linen closet and started to make the bed. In addition to the twin bed, there was a small bureau against one wall of the otherwise empty room. "Sorry, it's not much. We haven't had the time or money to fix up the guest bedrooms yet."

One corner of the bottom sheet kept popping off the mattress. The beer and wine Cassidy had been drinking all night didn't improve her dexterity.

"Here, let me do that. I don't need to be waited on." As she stepped back, Kye quickly and expertly tucked the sheets to military smoothness. Cassidy couldn't stop herself from visualizing him naked on the bed, herself beneath him, pinned by his masculine, sexy body. She shivered.

Kye turned to her. "It was truly my great good fortune to wander into that bar, Cassidy Luke." He locked eyes with hers and her stomach dropped. She moved toward him, her lips parting. He took her into his arms, leaned down and kissed her on the forehead.

Cassidy pulled back, confused. All night the sexual tension had whirred just below the surface. Surely it hadn't been all one-sided? He knew she and Ian weren't lovers, so what was the deal?

Again she reached for him, shutting her eyes and parting her lips in a very clear invitation. With her eyes closed, her head whirled from too much alcohol and she clung to him to keep from falling.

Gently but firmly he extracted himself from her arms. "I've

had a wee bit too much to drink, I'm afraid." His voice was apologetic. "Best if we get some sleep. Thank you again for your gracious hospitality."

The dismissal was clear. Here was the first guy since Ian to finally really grab her attention, and he didn't want her either. What was the deal? Stung, she said stiffly, "You're welcome. Sleep well."

Chapter Three

The next morning Cassidy woke to the smell of something wonderful. In retrospect she was glad Kye hadn't responded to her sexual invitation. What had she been thinking, with Ian downstairs? She'd known the guy all of four hours. In her defense, she had been completely sloshed. At least Kye's gentle refusal left her dignity intact.

The delicious aromas were making her mouth water. Something sweet was baking, and bacon was sizzling on the stove. Freshly brewed coffee rounded out the bouquet. Cassidy got up, threw on a T-shirt and shorts and hurried to the bathroom down the hall.

When she entered the kitchen, she found the table covered in one of the old white linen tablecloths her grandmother had given her many years before, and which she'd never found occasion to use. The table was already set for three.

Kye was standing at the stove. He turned toward her as she entered the kitchen. "Good morning. I just pulled together a little something from what I could find in the cabinets and fridge. I hope you don't mind."

"Oh, not at all." Cassidy moved toward the stove. "I didn't even know we had bacon."

"I found it in the freezer. I hope it's all right I took the liberty of throwing something together."

"Are you kidding? Better than all right. Breakfast around here usually consists of a cup of coffee and a piece of toast."

Kye leaned down, pulling open the old oven door, the hinges of which creaked from disuse. Cassidy didn't admit she'd never used the thing, not once in the six months since they'd been in the house. Kye removed a large muffin pan, filling the room with the scent of blueberry and melted butter. "I found a bag of blueberries in the freezer too. I poked around in the cabinets. You had all the ingredients I needed for muffins, so I just whipped together a batch."

"You made those from scratch?" Cassidy's mouth was watering.

"The only way to do it." Kye waved toward the table. "Sit down. I'll join you in just a second."

In short order he brought over the muffins, which he placed in a woven basket he'd lined with a tea towel. He slid the bacon onto a plate and brought over the coffeepot, pouring some into Cassidy's mug.

"Thanks." She smiled. "This is really nice of you. I should be the one doing all this, not you."

"Not at all." Kye smiled back, laugh lines radiating at the corners of his eyes. "It's my pleasure."

"I could get used to this." Cassidy took a muffin, the steam still rising off it, and bit into it. "Did you sleep okay on that old bed?"

"Like a baby."

Did he sleep naked? She bet he did.

A few moments later Ian walked into the kitchen, wearing only his pajama bottoms. His hair was spiked endearingly around his head and he looked incredibly sexy, but then, he always did. Cassidy noticed Kye watching him too, and she thought she detected a glimmer of lust. The idea was unsettling. What if Kye preferred Ian over her?

After all, his last relationship had been with a man. Perhaps he indulged in the occasional fling with a woman, but it was quite possible his primary focus was thoroughly masculine. Was she out of the running before she'd even had a chance?

Cut it out, she warned herself. He was there to help with the business plan, not to start a relationship with her, for God's sake. He was leaving in a day or two anyway. If he was attracted to Ian, it was only natural. With his tall, lean body, honey blond hair and golden brown eyes, he would be a catch for anyone, man or woman. Ian wasn't hers. She had no claim.

"The smell of cooking woke me up. I thought I was dreaming." Ian laughed. "Wow, what is all this? Cass?" He looked surprised.

Cassidy grinned. "I wish I could take the credit. The heavenly aromas woke me up too. I bet you didn't know we had all the ingredients to make blueberry muffins, huh? They're delicious too. If you hurry, I might not eat all of them before you get one."

Ian joined them at the table. When they were done eating, Kye poured himself a second cup of coffee and reached for the dirty plates, piling them neatly in a stack. "I'll just clean up the mess I made here. Shall we meet after that to go over the business records?"

"Sure, that sounds good. But you don't have to clean up. After all, you made it."

Kye shook his head. "I wouldn't hear of it. I'll be done in no time flat. In fact, if you want to shower or whatever, you can show me now where the records are, and I can begin to familiarize myself with the numbers while I wait for you."

"So you guys are good?" Ian pushed back from the table. "I can go finish the pendants?" Cassidy glanced at Ian. Wasn't he even the tiniest bit jealous? No, she thought with an inward sigh, he wasn't.

"You're excused," Kye said teasingly. "But later I'm going to want to sit down with you as well, to get a feel for the materials and workflow. From what Cassidy's told me so far, one of the weaknesses of this business is a failure to communicate. With such a small venture, you both need to have a good handle on all aspects of the business, even if it's not your area of expertise."

"So I'm supposed to know how to make jewelry?" Cassidy interjected.

"In a general sense, yes. If you understand the process and know what to look for, it makes you that much of a better salesperson when you take your product to market. You know firsthand what a good piece is and why it's good. The more you know about the product, the better off you and your company will be."

"You sound like one of those training videos on how to run your own business," Cassidy said. "Except I like your accent better."

Kye laughed. "Maybe I'll have to look into making one of those for my next project. Meanwhile, I've got dishes to wash." He jumped up, rapidly clearing the table, stacking everything like an expert waiter and whisking it to the sink.

Ian and Cassidy left the kitchen together. Cassidy followed Ian into the large living room that served as their combined office and studio. Glancing toward the kitchen, Ian spoke in an undertone. "Is that guy for real? Cooking, cleaning, that sexy accent, the buff bod and brains to boot? He's enough to give a guy a serious complex." He eyed her appraisingly. "I have to confess, last night when you brought him home I thought he was your date or something."

Cassidy shrugged, aware her cheeks were hot, annoyed that she was probably blushing. Kye had made it clear he was just passing through. And even if she had decided to go after him, she didn't need Ian's permission. Though they did actually consult one another from time to time about someone new they were thinking of dating. This usually resulted in the kiss of death for whoever was being considered, as Ian and Cassidy began to dissect their potential failings and all the things that would inevitably go wrong between them. Sometimes Cassidy thought that, though he didn't want her as a girlfriend, he didn't want her to have anyone else either. If she were honest, she felt the same way about him.

Ian's face creased into a frown. "I didn't realize we were in such dire financial straits. How come you didn't tell me before?"

Cassidy tried not to react defensively. "I didn't want you to worry. I'm supposed to handle that end of things. And until recently I was doing okay. It's just seemed to get away from me lately. We're growing too fast. Kye says that's a good thing, as long as we get some systems in place to manage the growth."

"Now you sound like him." Ian grinned. "Next thing I know you're going to be baking muffins."

"Don't hold your breath." They both laughed.

Cʒ

Kye and Cassidy spent several hours going over receipts, inventory, sales figures, online orders and wholesale orders. Cassidy was embarrassed as she handed him shoeboxes filled with receipts and papers she'd meant someday to file but had never found the time for.

Kye was full of praise for the online website she'd designed, as well as her photographs of the jewelry. He was not so impressed with her vague and periodic attempts to automate income and expense data, both for the internal books and tax records.

"They make software for this, you know," he said finally, after giving her a crash course in Accounting 101. "You don't have to do this all on your own. We'll go out this afternoon and get a good program. You spend a few hours familiarizing yourself with it. I'll help you set up the initial procedures. Within a day or two we'll have you operating like a real business. We'll get a tax software package as well, and start preparing your quarterly tax return."

Cassidy tried to take it all in. The truth was, she didn't want to become an accounting and tax expert, but she knew if she didn't do it, it wouldn't get done. Ian had more than enough to do just trying to keep up with demand.

Kye and Cassidy were side by side on the huge, faded, blue velvet sofa that had sat in Ian's great aunt's living room for fifty years, and was up for grabs when her estate was being divided among the cousins. Ian was ensconced on the other side of the room, lost in concentration as he bent over his work.

When Kye pointed to something in Cassidy's hands, his arm grazed her breast, causing a thrill of sensation to rush through her nerve endings. She couldn't control the small shiver of pleasure when his thickly muscled thigh pressed against her leg from time to time. She was also aware of Ian across the room, his blond head bent over his work.

After about an hour Ian stood, stretched and yawned. "I need some fresh air. I'm gonna take a walk. Anyone care to join me?" It being spring, the weather hadn't yet become oppressively hot and wet, as it soon would, dropping a muggy net over the city that wouldn't let up until October.

Kye looked toward Cassidy. "We probably should take a break. This is a lot to take in in one sitting." He stood. "If you'll excuse me, I think I'll take a shower. Then, if you've got a washer and dryer I could use, I would love to wash my stuff before I hit the road again."

Ian left for his walk, while Cassidy showed Kye the laundry room and got him fresh towels for his shower. She fantasized about slipping into the bathroom once he was in the shower, dropping her clothing and climbing in with him, but of course she would do no such thing.

Once she heard the sound of water running, Cassidy returned to the living room, settled herself against the plump, overstuffed sofa and called her sister, Jane. When Jane's voice mail answered, Cassidy let out a puff of frustration. Still, she left a message.

"Hi, Jane, I met this gorgeous guy. He's from Scotland, he's a musician and he's helping us with our business and he's got these incredible silver-gray eyes and Ian likes him too but he's only staying for a few days and I think I could fall in love with him. Call me."

CB

The lawn was mowed, the kitchen floor sparkled and quarterly tax returns had been prepared. Kye and Cassidy had gone grocery shopping together, Kye picking out what he needed for the meals he planned to make before he left. Cassidy told him he was going to make her fat with his homemade, delicious food, but that didn't stop her from eating it. Each morning he was up before either of them, breakfast on the stove, coffee brewed, a smile on his handsome face.

Both Ian and Cassidy agreed they were taking advantage of the guy—he was doing way more than he needed to just for using the spare bedroom, but every time they tried to stop him, he would smile that roguish smile and insist it was his pleasure.

When he wasn't working around the house or showing Cassidy how to use the new financial software, he would play his guitar, the warm, rich sound soothing. When they asked him what kind of music it was, Kye responded, "I guess you could say it's eclectic. A hodgepodge of genres I picked up from my travels—part blues, part Gaelic and Celtic ballad, part traditional English folk, part jazz."

He played complex, lush chords that were like nothing Cassidy had heard before. The music teased out emotions she hadn't known were hidden inside—sorrow, longing, joy, aching desperation—and presented them for inspection, turning them into something beautiful in the process. Ian too was moved by the music, and would invariably stop what he was doing to listen, his face going slack with pleasure.

That evening as the sun was setting, Ian and Cassidy were sitting together on the front porch, sipping beer. Kye had borrowed the car to attend to some personal business. Ian turned to Cassidy. "You know, he's the first guy who's actually worthy of you. Too bad he'll only be around another couple of days."

"He'd be worthy of you too," she retorted with a grin. "His last love affair was a guy, you know."

Ian raised his eyebrows and shook his head, though he said nothing. He'd had his share of bisexual dalliances in the past, of which Cassidy was aware. She felt a sudden unpleasant pang of jealousy at the possibility of these two gorgeous men hooking up. For the first time she was relieved Kye was leaving, at least on some level. In a surprisingly short time he'd worked his way into their affections, not only because of all he had done for them, but just because of who he was. She would miss him.

"Maybe we could convince him to stay." Ian's thoughts were apparently on the same track.

Another tendril of jealousy snaked its way through her innards, but Cassidy shook it off. "He's got this audition thing in Austin."

"Yeah, I know." Ian was quiet a moment. "Maybe he'd stay longer if we had something to offer him. Something to entice him to stay in Houston." He turned his gaze squarely on Cassidy.

She couldn't help it—whenever he looked directly at her like that she felt a rush of desire. Of all the men she'd been with, he was the only one who could make her blush just with his stare. It was as if he looked past her flesh and bone, straight into her soul. He knew secrets she'd never told anyone, not even him. He controlled her completely at those moments, though she doubted he was aware of his own power.

She looked away. Ian, oblivious of his affect on her, continued. "What if we offered him something that made it worth his while to stay?"

"Like what? We haven't got anything of worth except the business."

"Exactly."

"What do you mean?"

"I mean, we could offer him a job. Invite him to join the company as our finance guy. Our money man." Ian began to speak rapidly, which he did when he was excited about an idea. "It would free you up to do the stuff you really like—the photo layouts and the marketing. What do you think?"

"I think you're going awfully fast with someone we just met." Despite her protest, Cassidy's heart quickened, and not, she knew, because of the strength Kye brought to the business. Cassidy squelched her unrequited desire. "Though I have to admit, it's amazing how much he's helped me in just a few days to understand the business end of things, and to put procedures in place to help us going forward. If he stayed, he could go with us to the bank next week. I know he'd say all the right things to get the line of credit."

"Yeah. Too bad we can't pay him for shit." Ian sighed. "He's probably not the kind of guy who could settle down to something like this. I mean, he hasn't so far."

"Yeah," Cassidy agreed. Kye, like the two of them, considered himself a free spirit, though he took it further than either of them, actually wandering the world in search of adventure and, sometimes, romance. At twenty-eight, he had told them, he'd yet to really fall in love, though he'd let his heart get bruised a time or two.

Ian took a long drink of his beer. "I wonder if he can even work legally in this country. Does he have a green card or whatever?"

Cassidy's mind began to race with possibilities, some related to the business, some decidedly not. "Actually he doesn't need a green card. He's an American citizen."

"Really? I thought he was from Scotland. The accent, his stories—"

"He's Scottish all right, but he was born here in the U.S. His mother is American. She met his dad when he was here studying at a university. They had Kye while still living here, but then moved to Edinburgh when he was only two. He's always maintained a dual citizenship."

Ian shot her a look. "You seem to know a lot about him, not that I'm surprised."

Cassidy raised an eyebrow, her heart quickening with a longing she barely permitted herself to recognize. "What's it to you? Do I detect a note of jealousy?" She kept her tone light.

Ian laughed. "Yeah, right."

Kye chose that moment to drive up, parking in the driveway and emerging from the car. He reached into the backseat and pulled out several sacks of groceries. Cassidy admired his long, smooth stride as he walked toward them.

"I picked up some fresh ears of corn at the farmers' market." Kye held up the bag. "It'll go well with the dish I have planned."

"You do too much." Cassidy didn't want to take advantage of Kye, though she loved having prepared meals, and he genuinely seemed to enjoy cooking.

"She's right, Kye. You've done way more than just help us with the business. You're totally spoiling us. We were just talking about how we don't know what we're going to do when you go."

"We were thinking," Cassidy added.

"That maybe," Ian interjected, "you could stay a while longer?"

"Maybe a lot longer?" Cassidy finished hopefully.

Kye looked from one to the other, tilting his head quizzically. "I've had a terrific time, truly I have. You helped me get past a bit of a rough patch, emotionally speaking. The distraction was just what I needed." Cassidy knew he was talking about the guy he'd followed to Texas from Greece. "However," he continued, "I make it a policy never to overstay my welcome. You graciously agreed to let me stay for the week, and in return I've tried to do what I can to be of service to you.

"Now it's time to move on. I have this audition thing, as I mentioned. I'm between jobs at the moment, and I would like to find some kind of steady work. This band, while not my ideal, should do nicely until the next thing pops up. They do covers, mostly, and earn decent money, at least as far as local bands go."

"Is that what you really want, to be in a cover band? With your kind of talent, it seems to me you'd be wasted on a group like that," Ian observed.

"Well, thank you for the compliment." Kye shrugged. "To answer your question—is it what I want permanently? No. But so far nothing better has leaped out at me, you know? I've rarely held a job for more than a year—I'm easily bored." He grinned. "I don't do well in structured environments. I think I would wither away to ashes if I had to work in an office. Not to mention, I always end up wanting to take control of everything, not a trait especially admired by one's superiors."

"What if," Ian began.

"You found something better?" Cassidy offered.

"Such as?" Kye waited.

"Ian Tanner Designs," Cassidy blurted. "We want you to stay. We want you to join the company, as our finance guy. You already know more about how to run it in three days than I could learn in a year."

"Yeah." Ian's voice was eager. "We can't really pay much—"

"Yet," Cassidy interjected. "But we want you—for the business I mean."

"And because we genuinely like and admire you." Ian looked as hopeful as a puppy waiting for a treat.

Kye sat on the top stair of the porch. "I don't know what to say." He ran one hand through his hair and pursed his lips in thought. "It's a tempting offer. I wasn't bullshitting you about the potential worth of your venture. You're a phenomenal talent, Ian. It's just a matter of time and handling before you go national, I'm sure of it."

Ian beamed. Kye shook his head. "But I can't really see myself working for someone. No offense, but I don't like that whole scene. I've done it because I've had to, but like I said before, I start to chafe after a while. Just the term employee sends shivers of dread through me. Even wonderful people like you—I just can't see myself reporting to you, no matter how informal the arrangement."

"What if..." Cassidy hoped Ian would be behind her on what she was about to say. "What if instead of working for us, you worked with us?"

"What are you saying?"

"A percentage of the business. A share of the profits. Part ownership." She looked at Ian, who, to her relief, was nodding in enthusiastic agreement.

"You're joking." Kye's tone was emphatic.

"No. Serious."

"Cassidy." Kye shook his head. "Your generosity is truly touching, but we've known one another less than a week. You can't offer me something of such magnitude. I couldn't possibly accept that. I've done nothing yet to earn it."

"Do you like being here?" Determination filled Ian's tone.

"Very much."

"Would you enjoy working with us? Not for us, but with us, on this venture? Living with us? Would you perhaps consider giving it a go for a month or so? Maybe we could work up an informal agreement, something we could all be comfortable with." Ian gestured with his empty beer bottle. "You could stay a while and see how it goes. Then we could talk it over again, see where you're at, where we're at. What do you say? Wouldn't this be more fun than living in some crummy flophouse and playing covers in college dorms while drunk kids puke around you?"

"When you put it like that..."

"So you will? Please?" Cassidy leapt from her chair and impulsively put her arms around him.

"Okay, okay. You've convinced me." Kye laughed, hugging Cassidy back. She found she didn't want to let go, but forced herself to step back. "I'm not yet ready to accept a share of the business, but I'll stay a while longer. At least long enough to go with you to the bank next week. How's that sound?"

"Like we've got ourselves a deal." Ian slapped his thighs enthusiastically. "Leave that corn for tomorrow. Let's go out to dinner instead to celebrate our new relationship."

Chapter Four

Ian sipped his wine, observing the pair. Cassidy leaned her head close, her lovely green eyes focused on his face as Kye talked. It struck him as an intimate gesture, and though he had no right, he was jealous.

He wasn't sure exactly how he felt about things. He knew he'd surprised Cassidy with his suggestion that Kye stay. He'd surprised himself even more. Though he considered himself passively bisexual—he didn't actively seek out guys for sex, but *was* attracted to certain guys—it had been years since he'd been involved with another man.

Over the past few days, watching Cassidy and Kye interact, he'd experienced a host of strange feelings. He was pretty sure nothing sexual was going on between them—yet. But now that they'd invited Kye to stay, surely it was only a matter of time before those two got together.

Not for the first time, he wondered what it was that kept him from falling in love with Cassidy. Was he holding out for the next best thing? Was he afraid to settle, to get tied down to the wrong person? What was it about the two of them, Cassidy and himself, that had backfired when they had segued from friends to lovers?

Watching her now, he recalled the first time he'd seen her. He'd been with Angela at the time, one in a string of failed relationships after Kim. He'd first noticed Cassidy kneeling by the edge of the pool, a small camera in her hands, ignoring everyone and everything around her as she snapped pictures of the ground.

He'd been curious, and coming closer, realized she was taking pictures of the brightly colored mosaic tiles inlaid around the edge of the pool. His shadow fell over her, and she glanced up with eyes as clear as green glass. Her face was surrounded by a cascade of coppery hair that shimmered in the sunlight. Her skin had a milky rose-splashed glow. She was as lovely then as she was now.

From the beginning they'd been kindred spirits. Like him, she didn't want to be tied down by anyone. Early on Ian had learned to shield his heart. It wasn't that he didn't love Cassidy—he did. But he'd learned his lesson all too well with Kim. It was better to stay friends with a woman he cared about. Sex seemed to ruin things every time.

He had started out as just friends with Kim, too, and look where that had ended up. He'd been twenty-one but still wet behind the ears, sexually and romantically speaking. Kim was two years older and far more experienced. She'd had a boyfriend when they first met, and he hadn't permitted himself to think of her as a potential lover.

But when she'd broken up with the guy and shown up at Ian's apartment with a bottle of champagne, he'd never looked back. He'd tumbled head over feet for the lovely brunette, proposing to her after only six months. He'd been so sure she was THE ONE in all capital letters.

Yet from the moment he'd slipped the diamond ring on her finger, he'd felt the first stirrings of disquiet. He was so young, after all. What if he was making a mistake? Why had he been in such a hurry? *Was* she the one? What if he was settling, just because she was there? Unfortunately his fears eventually culminated into a self-fulfilling prophecy.

He began to notice her faults, which seemed to be

magnified under the glass of their engagement. He knew it wasn't fair, but he began to feel she'd rushed him into the relationship. Little by little he started to withdraw, though she was the one who finally broke it off.

"I need a man who can commit. You're not that guy, Ian. When you grow up, give me a call."

He'd been stung but relieved. What had he been thinking? Marriage was overrated. His own parents had been miserable, staying together, it seemed to him, only because each feared to be alone. He'd never seen them kiss or exchange an endearment. They barely looked at one another, except when they were fighting. Once after he'd moved out, Ian had dared to ask his mother why she put up with his dad, who got mean when he drank, and he drank often.

"We've been married twenty-four years, Ian," she answered sharply. "You don't just throw away a lifetime of commitment. I wouldn't know how to start over. Anyway, he's not so bad, when he's sober."

Was that all there was to look forward to? It being "not so bad"? He knew why his father stayed in what seemed to be a loveless marriage—his mother waited on him hand and foot, in addition to holding down a job and raising Ian and his little sister. His father worked too, though he was fired every couple of years due to excessive absences while he slept off the latest drinking binge.

After Kim, Ian drifted, often going for months at a time without dating anyone. Angela had just been one in a series of casual girlfriends. In retrospect, he realized she'd cheated on him because he was emotionally unavailable to her. In that regard he'd been acting, he thought with horror, like his father, though at least he wasn't a drunk.

Cassidy was different. From the beginning she never demanded anything of him. There was no hidden agenda to hook him, to get engaged, to find a suitable mate to father her children. She, like him, didn't want to be tied down. It was what had connected them from the first. That, and their shared love of color and design. She understood and encouraged his work, even pooling her resources with his to get the business going.

The brief interlude as lovers had been a nearly fatal mistake. He'd felt the old tensions and worries of feeling trapped and tied down begin to rear their heads. Though he didn't want to, he found himself shutting down, picking fights, taking stock and finding her wanting. He knew the problem lay with himself. Somehow he had lost, or had never had, the capacity to connect, to surrender himself on a level deep enough to allow true love to reach him.

What a relief it had been when they both agreed to ease their way back into a platonic relationship. The irony of it all was that with Cassidy, unlike the other women he'd been involved with, he had withdrawn from the sexual relationship not because he didn't want her, but because he wanted her too much. He knew in his heart of hearts if they continued to be lovers, it was only a matter of time before he pushed her away— before he lost her forever.

The thought of losing her was more than he could handle, though he'd never let her know the depth of his feelings. She had been content, even eager, to return to their earlier friendship. He had half expected her to refuse—to break up with him for good when he'd said they worked better as friends.

The fact that she hadn't had confirmed his suspicions that they had been on the wrong path as lovers. After all, if she'd really loved him, why did she so easily agree to let go of the sex? He had been right to pull back. Cassidy, like him, would never be able to commit. In that, though it made him sad to admit it, they were kindred as well.

Yet he knew he couldn't bear not to have her in his life. He was glad they shared the deed and mortgage on the house—it was probably as close to getting married as they'd ever get, and it tied them together, if only financially. By the same token, he was glad she was part of the business.

Now they'd added a new partner to the business. But was he more than that? Was he a potential lover for Cassidy? The men she'd brought by over the years had never threatened Ian. He knew almost before Cass that she'd lose interest in a week or a month, and invariably she had.

But Kye was different. It wasn't just that he was very good looking or spoke with that marvelous accent or the way he possessed everyone around him when he played his guitar. There was something about him. When he listened, he seemed to listen with his entire being. Something deep in his eyes seemed to say, "I know you, and I want to know you better."

Cassidy was as drawn to Kye as he was—more so. For the first time he had to consider the very real possibility that someone might actually steal Cassidy's heart. Was he just going to stand by and let it happen?

CR

She hadn't planned it, though she'd fantasized about it a dozen times in the two weeks since Kye had moved in. A little warning bell in her head told Cassidy to keep things with Kye nonsexual, but her own desire drowned it out.

Things were complicated enough with Ian. Secretly she pined for him, though her pride wouldn't allow her to admit it. Even to Jane she played down just how in love she was with the man who had rejected her. It was humiliating to admit to anyone else how much she still wanted him.

Kye was the first man to take her out of herself. He was the first man since Ian who had completely captured her attention. Though he remained the perfect gentleman, she sensed his interest as well. When they worked in close proximity, he would brush her arm or touch her thigh and invariably it sent a thrill of warmth surging through her. She wanted him, oh yes, she did.

That morning Ian was at a jewelry show downtown and wouldn't be back for several hours. Kye was looking especially sexy in a dark blue T-shirt, his jeans molding nicely around the sexy package at his crotch.

They were sitting side by side on the sofa, as they often did, her laptop between them, going over design ideas for the new catalog. Kye traced the silver band she wore, drawing his finger along her hand to her forearm.

"Pretty ring." His touch made her shiver.

"Ian made it."

"I figured." His hand remained on her arm. They looked at one another and suddenly all the longing she felt for both Ian and Kye seemed to merge. Her skin was burning beneath his hand, her heart thumping as he leaned over and kissed her.

After a moment he pulled back. "I've been wanting to do that forever," he whispered huskily. "I hope it's okay. I mean, you and Ian—"

"Are just friends," she interjected, at once embarrassed at the bitterness that had entered her tone.

"Aye, so you both say." Kye smiled, his eyes kind, perhaps even a little sad. "So then, may I kiss you again?"

"Yes." Her eyes fluttered shut as she offered her face up to his. Carefully he set the laptop aside. Then he kissed her until she was breathless. He slid one strong arm beneath her thighs and scooped her onto his lap so she was facing him, her legs straddling his.

Again he kissed her, the tip of his tongue slipping like hot silk between her lips. She had fantasized about this since the first moment she'd laid eyes on him. It hardly seemed real now that it was actually happening.

Cassidy was wearing a button-down, sleeveless blouse. Her breasts were bare beneath the soft cotton. Fingers trembling, she unbuttoned the first button while Kye watched with hungry eyes. She undid the second one, aware she was breathing too fast.

Oh God, what am I doing, what am I doing, what am I doing? But she didn't stop. She couldn't stop. It had been so long since she'd thrilled to the touch of another man. Ian, she had often told herself ruefully, when yet another date turned out to be a dud, had ruined her for other men.

Kye drove all thoughts from her mind as he pushed the shirt from her shoulders. "Saints preserve us," he marveled. "Aren't you a lovely sight to behold?"

Cassidy ducked her head to hide her pleased embarrassment, reaching for the metal buttons of his fly. Kye arched his hips obligingly to give her better access. At the same time he reached for hers, pulling at the snap and dragging the zipper down in one deft movement.

She lifted herself from him long enough to slide out of her shorts. She was wearing white lace panties, glad for their cover, at least for the moment. Kye, less shy than she, pushed his jeans and underwear down to his thighs, revealing a hard, straight shaft that, despite her nervousness, made her mouth water with desire.

Her heart was beating so loud she just knew Kye could hear it. He pulled her close, so his cock nestled up against her lace-covered cleft. Dropping his head, he tugged at her nipple with his teeth, drawing a moan of lust from her. Her panties were wet, her clit throbbing.

His mouth still on her breast, Kye slipped two fingers beneath the lace, pushing it aside. One finger entered her wetness and she moaned, unable to stop herself from grinding against it.

"Lord, I want you, Cassidy. I do. But I like you too much to take advantage." For one horrible second she thought he was going to stop. If he did, she'd end up raping him, if a woman could rape a man.

He continued, "We need to use protection. I've been with a lot of people. I always practice safe sex."

Cassidy knew he was right, though she wanted nothing more than to lower herself over that beautiful member, not stopping until she'd taken him to the hilt. To her surprise he didn't push her away and head off to find his backpack. Instead, with her still balanced over him, he lifted his hips, reached in the back pocket of the pants that were now at knee level and pulled out a slim black wallet.

He pushed his jeans the rest of the way off and kicked them aside. Flipping open the wallet, he extracted a condom packet. She watched as he tore the wrapper and slipped the thin latex over his gorgeous cock.

"Now, where were we?"

Cassidy reminded him by repositioning herself over his shaft, pulling the flimsy lace of her panties aside. She was so wet she barely noticed the condom.

He felt like heaven, filling her completely. His hands on her hips, he guided her body, moving with her in erotic tandem. He began swiveling in such a way it sent spirals of shivery pleasure hurtling through her.

"Oh," she moaned breathlessly. "Whatever you're doing, don't stop. Please, don't ever, ever stop."

He teased her, bringing her to the edge of climax, only to still, his eyes burning as he watched her shudder and writhe over him, desperate for him to continue. When she could stand it no more, she cried, "*Please.* Don't stop this time, I'm begging you." He obliged, ratcheting the intensity until he was slamming into her, his fingers digging into her hips. The tendons stood out on his neck, his breathing labored, his dark hair falling wild over his eyes.

Cassidy fell forward against him, her hair whipping his chest as she shuddered and jerked, experiencing an intense, extended orgasm that gripped her and just wouldn't let go. When at last the spasms overtaking her body subsided, she lay limp against Kye's chest, his cock still buried deep inside her. She could feel the slow, steady thud of his heart against hers. His arms circled her body, calloused fingers stroking her bare back.

When she finally found the strength to move, Cassidy rolled off his lap, collapsing on the sofa beside him. What, she found herself thinking, was she going to tell Ian?

ℭ

Cassidy was making her rounds in the city with a new batch of Ian's latest pieces. It was late afternoon and Ian had been hard at it since early that morning, with only a short break for lunch, a chicken salad sandwich and fresh lemonade courtesy of their new tenant.

Now that they had the gems, copper, silver and gold that he needed, he was desperately trying to fill a flood of incoming orders. He'd been working so hard his fingers had begun to cramp and his back muscles were in knots.

Kye entered the studio just as Ian was flexing his back in an effort to relieve the aching muscles between his shoulder blades. Without saying anything, Kye moved behind him, strong fingers kneading the precise spot that ached. Ian leaned gratefully against his fingers.

Ian closed his eyes, letting himself drift as Kye worked his magic. "You work too hard, lad."

Ian revived at the reminder. "I have no choice. We got backed up waiting for the materials. I'm trying to make up for lost time."

Kye stepped beside him, his hand still resting against Ian's back. With his other hand, he picked up a bracelet made from cultured pearls and glass beads threaded on copper strands. "This is beautiful. It reminds me of the crest of a wave in a Japanese painting." Ian smiled, pleased with the description.

"You know." Kye was thoughtful. "It might be time to get you an assistant. Someone to help with the bead work, the soldering and repetitive tasks."

Ian was keenly aware of Kye's hand still on his back. He leaned against it. "Can we afford that?"

"I want to see how the end-of-the-month numbers play out. Would you be okay with bringing someone on board? I know you creative types are very protective of your designs. I'm thinking an apprentice, someone who's hungry to learn the craft. Just part time, at least to start."

"I think that would be okay," Ian answered. He had half expected Kye to volunteer himself. No doubt he'd be as good at jewelry making as he was at everything else.

Kye stepped back and Ian at once missed the warmth of his hand. Kye was appraising the large living room that doubled as office and studio. "You need your own space—somewhere without the distractions of the office and home. We might want to think about partitioning off this area, giving you the space you need to work without interruption, or perhaps moving Cassidy out altogether."

They talked about possible plans, Kye as usual very focused on the business. Ian wanted to ask him straight out what was going on between him and Cassidy, but didn't quite have the nerve. He knew *something* was going on, though

Cassidy hadn't offered any details. Still, he wasn't blind.

He had noticed a subtle shift in her behavior lately, and wondered if she and Kye had become lovers. With other men she dated, she usually ended up confiding in him about their sexual relationship, though only after it had failed. Somehow he doubted any kind of liaison with Kye could fail.

His back twinged again and he reached for the knotted muscle.

"Let me do that," Kye offered. He'd been sitting perched on the edge of Ian's large worktable. "Come over to the sofa. You've definitely earned a break."

Ian followed him to the oversized sofa, stretching himself out on it with a contented sigh. "Take off your shirt, I can do a better job that way." Kye tone was casual, as if he massaged men every day.

Ian complied, pulling his T-shirt over his head and dropping it to the floor beside the sofa. Kye sat next to him, kneading the knotted muscles between his shoulder blades. After a moment his hands slid lower, slipping just beneath the waist of Ian's shorts.

Strong fingers moved in sure strokes over Ian's back. It tickled at first and sometimes hurt as he pressed deep into twisted muscle. His muscles softened and unknotted as they yielded to the skilled, sensual touch.

After several languorous minutes during which Kye continued his deep massage, Ian melted into the sofa. Kye's touch lightened, his fingers gliding along Ian's sides. If he'd been less relaxed it would have tickled.

Ian was wearing cutoff shorts he'd made from a pair of old blue jeans. Kye straddled the backs of Ian's bare thighs. "You have a very strong back," he remarked. "Are you a swimmer?"

"I used to be," Ian managed to murmur. "On the swim team in college." He was aroused by Kye's body over his, Kye's strong thighs gripping his own. He was sporting an erection and was glad Kye couldn't see it beneath him.

Kye's fingers swept lower, again slipping below the waist of Ian's shorts. This time they slipped beneath the elastic of his underwear. Ian was too relaxed to move or protest. More than that, he was aroused by the touch.

Kye ran his hands over Ian's ass. Ian wanted to roll over and pull him down, but didn't dare. His mind could barely process what was happening, but his body was way ahead of it, his cock rigid beneath him.

Were Kye and he going to become lovers? What would Cass say? Would she be jealous? Or would she want to join in?

As if she'd been waiting to be remembered before appearing, Ian heard the sound of the front door opening, and a moment later Cassidy's sweet, low voice calling, "Hi, y'all. I'm home."

Kye's hands were withdrawn, the weight of his body lifted. Ian pulled himself upright in time to see Cassidy enter the room, a quizzical smile on her face.

"Have I interrupted something?" She looked pointedly at Ian's bare torso.

"I was just giving Ian a massage." Kye gave her a dazzling smile. "Would you care to join us?"

Chapter Five

Her cheeks were flushed, though whether from the heat outside or what she'd witnessed, Ian couldn't say. "A massage, huh?" Cassidy arched one delicate brow. Ian tried to decide if the smile on her lips was sly or innocent.

Embarrassment, confusion and lust jumbled through his brain. He could still feel the imprint of Kye's strong fingers gliding sensually over his ass. His neck felt hot and he knew he was blushing. He stole a glance at Kye, who was leaning back in a relaxed position against the velvet sofa, an enigmatic smile on his face.

"Boy, it's hot out there," Cassidy said. Ian couldn't help but wonder if there was a subtext—boy, it's hot *in here.* She dropped the two heavy cases that contained samples of Ian's jewelry designs. "So much for Houston's two weeks of spring." She lifted her hair, drawing Ian's eye to her long, slender neck.

Cassidy was wearing a dark blue sundress that offset her milky smooth skin and showed off her shapely legs. Ian noted Kye, too, was eyeing her appreciatively. Now jealousy rose to the fore in the stew of emotions swirling through his psyche. Kye, he was suddenly certain, had seen the bare breasts beneath the silk. He'd caressed those sweet round globes, licked and nibbled her perfect rosy nipples, his tongue sliding down to seek the soft petals of her sex...

Cassidy took a step forward and then stopped. She seemed

to be weighing something in her mind, but whatever it was didn't make it to her lips. "I'm going to take a shower. I'll catch up with y'all later." She walked through the room toward the stairs, climbing them quickly.

When she was gone, Kye turned to Ian. "Do you want to tell me about it?" His voice was gentle and coaxing.

"About what?" Ian refused to understand.

"What's really going on between you two? Cassidy assures me you're just friends. You say the same. But that's not the feeling I'm getting, not by a long shot. If I'm in the middle, creating a mess, I want to know. Talk to me."

Ian slumped back onto the sofa and ran his hands through his hair. "There's not much to tell," he lied. "We're just friends. We were more once, briefly, but it didn't work out."

Kye touched his thigh, those piercing gray eyes penetrating his soul. Ian looked away. At the same time, despite himself, his cock responded to the touch.

"'Just friends' don't usually buy a house together, or start a business together." Kye raised his eyebrows.

"Yeah, well." Ian shrugged.

"You're in love with her, aren't you?"

"What?" Ian turned to stare at Kye, his mouth forming the words to deny it. Yet he didn't. Hearing someone else say it out loud was unsettling, to say the least. He'd been telling himself forever that he loved her, but wasn't *in* love with her. Yet watching Kye and Cassidy over these past few weeks, increasingly certain they were becoming more than friends, had forced him to reevaluate his feelings.

"She's in love with you, too, you know, if that makes it any easier."

Ian's heart skipped several beats. He shook his head. "If that's so, why is she having sex with you?" Jesus, he hadn't meant to say that. It was none of his business if they were or weren't. Well, he'd said it—there was no taking it back. He stared at Kye, silently daring him to deny it.

"She's a lovely woman. I won't lie to you—we have made love several times, only after she assured me you and she were not romantically involved. But since then we've begun to talk, really talk, and Ian, she's in love with you. She stays 'just friends' because she thinks that's what you want. She thinks it's the only way she can be around you. She's afraid if she presses the issue, you'll leave her."

Ian sat frozen. The image of Kye and Cassidy, naked, their bodies pressed together, Cassidy with her head thrown back, her lovely hair over the pillow, her soft, lithe body crushed beneath Kye's rose like a flame in Ian's mind. Then Kye's words slipped past the fire ring of jealousy burning in his brain.

She's in love with you... She's in love with you...

No. She wasn't. They'd discussed it, calmly, rationally, both admitting their relationship had become strained and difficult once they'd become lovers. It was so much easier to be friends. The ease, the simplicity of it, was surely better than the sticky confusion that invariably resulted when sex entered the mix.

So why was his heart lurching and twisting like someone was gripping it in their fist? *She's in love with you...* No, she couldn't be. She was Kye's lover now. He'd *admitted* it, right to Ian's face. They had made love. Kye had seized what Ian had been afraid to take. Kye wasn't afraid of the complications. Kye was more of a man, Ian knew with sudden, sickening clarity, than he was.

Kye interrupted his tortured thoughts. "Cassidy's an amazing woman. She's sensual and passionate. She has so much love to give. I didn't plan to seduce her, if that's what you're thinking. But you should know something about me. I've learned that life is too short and too precious to deny ourselves what can make us happy. I try to make it a point to tell the truth and to live in a way that makes me comfortable with myself.

"I'm a lot like the two of you, really. I've never been ready to settle down. I keep thinking the next great experience is just around the corner—be it a new place, new music, a new lover. I don't want to presume here, and you tell me if I'm wrong, but maybe, just maybe, you've held Cassidy at arm's length because you're still searching too. Looking for that next best thing."

And now I've lost it...lost her... It took another man, right in my own house, right under my nose, to make me see that.

Kye must have read the pain on his face. "Hey, it's okay. It's all good. We've more than enough love between the three of us to work this through. I'm not taking your love from you. I would never do that. I wouldn't want to. I desire her, yes." He touched Ian's bare thigh again. "I desire *you* as well. You're a very handsome, very sexy man."

Ian stared down at Kye's hand but didn't pull away. It had been several years since he'd been with another man. He'd never gone all the way, but he'd done some pretty serious experimenting, including oral sex, both giving and receiving. It had been hot and he'd been turned on, not only by the compelling attraction of a hard cock, but by his own daring.

Yet he'd always stopped short of an emotional connection with another guy. This, he had assured himself, was what made him straight with bi-tendencies, rather than gay. He would never actually fall for a man, not in the way he would and had for a woman.

He looked at Kye, at his clear gray eyes and his sensuous lips and the broad curve of his strong shoulders. He looked again at Kye's hand, the fingers of which were massaging his leg.

"You want me, too, don't you, Ian?" Kye drew his hand up along Ian's leg, the fingers slipping under his shorts, moving dangerously close to his crotch. Ian's cock strained and his breath caught in his throat.

There was a heat in his neck that moved along to the tips of his ears. Reflexively he opened his mouth to deny it, but then closed it. Almost against his will, he leaned toward Kye, compelled by the man's sensual magnetism. Ian couldn't help himself—his gaze dropped lower, to the sizable bulge in Kye's jeans. An image of himself kneeling between Kye's knees, taking the man's cock between his lips, seared his thoughts like a brand.

Kye turned those knowing eyes on him, the corners of his mouth lifting with the hint of a smile. Ian felt as transparent as water, as if Kye could see his thoughts like stones on the bottom of a clear pool. Aware he was blushing, he turned away.

Cassidy stood beneath the shower spray with her eyes closed, the image of Ian, bare-chested, his eyes sliding away from hers when she walked in on them. He'd looked startled, flustered, caught in the act. Kye's assertion he'd been giving Ian a massage was probably true, but she could tell whatever had been going on hadn't been entirely innocent.

In spite of the jealous feelings wending their way through her gut, at the same time she was burning with curiosity over what precisely had gone down between the two men. Had Ian been the one to instigate things? Whatever "things" were.

For all she knew, what she'd walked in on was as innocent as it appeared. Ian's shoulder muscles often ached when he sat too long hunched over his work, lost in concentration. Kye must have noticed and offered to help.

Or…or they were carrying on their own secret, torrid affair, having hot male/male sex while she was out hauling those heavy jewelry cases all over town. Kye was *hers*, damn it. She got there first.

She lathered her long hair and couldn't help but laugh at herself. She was jealous of *both* of them. She was possessive of both of them, when in fact she was in a relationship with neither. Not only that, she was definitely making assumptions based on very little. Yes, she knew Ian had dabbled with guys in the past, but it had been a long time, not that that meant anything.

Still, she had to admit, if he were going to fall for a guy, Kye would definitely be the one. Handsome, sexy, fun, easygoing and someone who was becoming a true friend to them both.

Cassidy climbed out of the shower and dried herself before the full-length mirror. She imagined the two men naked, locked in a sweaty, masculine embrace, muscles gleaming, cocks colliding...

Where would she fit in if the two guys started something? She stared at herself, noting her imperfections, balancing them against her sex appeal and finally turning away. "I want them both—so help me, I want them both."

Kye McClellan was a free spirit. That's how he described himself. Though he wasn't afraid to fall in love, and indeed had been in love several times over the years, he never felt compelled to stay in a relationship beyond its proper time.

People changed, situations altered and he instinctively knew when it was time to move on. He tried his best not to leave broken hearts behind, but he knew it was better to go than to stay in something that wasn't meant to be.

Watching the interaction between Ian and Cassidy over these past weeks, however, had drawn him up sharply in his introspections. The fact they were in love with each other was blindingly obvious, apparently to everyone except themselves. It was clear to Kye the two of them were meant to be together.

He realized with a clarity that left him terribly lonely, that he, too, had spent his life running the moment things got too intense or didn't work out just as he hoped. Was Derek a case in point? He would think about it later.

Now he watched Ian retrieve his T-shirt and pull it over his head. He'd felt Ian's reaction to his touch. He knew Ian was attracted to him, but was unsure of the extent. Jesus, he wanted them both. He hadn't planned this.

Though Cassidy was a beauty, he hadn't expected the passion or his own strong reaction to her. And Ian—what delightful unexplored possibilities remained between the two of them.

Between the three of them?

Ian stood, his face now smoothed into a neutral expression. "I guess I'd better finish those pearl cluster rings I've been working on. Cass wants to get them up on the site by the weekend."

Kye said nothing. He too stood and followed Ian to his worktable. Ian picked up a completed ring and handed it to Kye. "That's lovely." He held it up to the light. "What are the red stones?"

"Those are briolette garnets. The ring is made from oxidized silver and I group the garnets and drop pearls on top. This one was actually Cassidy's design. She's very creative. Of course, being a photographer, she has an excellent eye."

Kye heard the proprietary pride in Ian's voice and smiled. No question about it, this man was in love. He could deny it all he liked—just her name was enough to spark the love light in his eyes.

Love.

He thought he'd fallen in love with Derek in Greece—the kind of headlong, crazy love that rarely lasts. He'd foolishly believed Derek was in love with him too. He understood later Derek was in love with the adventure and the taboo of stepping past the rigid boundaries set by his family. Boundaries, it later turned out, that hemmed him firmly in place once he returned to the States and the controlling father who held the purse strings. Kye shook his memories away. Derek was the past now—history.

Both men turned to watch Cassidy as she came down the stairs. Her wet hair was the color of burnished bronze threaded with copper. She was dressed in a white T-shirt and dark blue shorts of thick, soft cotton. Her feet were bare. Kye wanted to take her then and there. He glanced at Ian, whose hungry expression indicated the same desire.

"I'm starving," she announced, apparently unaware of her affect on the two men, though somehow Kye doubted this.

Still, he was hungry too. He ordered his cock to go back to sleep. "Hey. Why don't we have a picnic? Ian, you could finish those rings while Cassidy and I whip up something."

"Let's barbeque," Cassidy suggested. "And I'll make a pitcher of frozen strawberry daiquiris."

"Watch out for Cass's strawberry daiquiris." Ian laughed. "You think you're drinking a slushie but they'll knock you on your ass."

"My kind of drink. We can use the last of those fresh strawberries." Kye turned to Cassidy. "Where's the grill kept? I didn't notice one out back."

"Somewhere in the garage, right, Ian?" Cassidy looked to Ian for confirmation.

Ian shrugged. "Not sure."

"Well, I think it's in there, behind all the boxes and crap. There should be a bag of charcoal somewhere too and some lighter fluid. We haven't used it yet since we moved here so I'm not sure."

"Shouldn't be too hard to find."

He left Cassidy in the kitchen gathering ingredients for the drinks and went out back toward the old freestanding garage. It didn't take long to find the grill, though it did take some maneuvering to get it past the stacks of boxes, the two bicycles and what looked like a broken washing machine. Kye made a mental note to tackle the garage once the weather cooled.

He stopped where he stood. Once the weather cooled? Did he really think he'd still be here come fall? Not usually one to obsess over the future, instead content to let it reveal itself, he shrugged, telling himself he would know in time.

He found a half-full bag of charcoal inside the grill, along with a tin of lighter fluid. In short order he had a fire going, with the coals heaped in a nice pyramid. Returning to the kitchen, he set about marinating the chicken breasts in olive oil, garlic, fresh lemon and spices.

He accepted the big-bowled wineglass Cassidy had filled with the frozen drink and sipped it. "Delicious," he pronounced, as they clinked glasses. He made a salad while Cassidy went to find a blanket for their picnic.

When everything was ready, Cassidy called out, "Ian, come and eat."

The three of them settled on the blanket, with plates piled with grilled chicken and fresh salad, their glasses filled with the frozen rum drink. Both Cassidy and Kye were on their seconds, Ian on his first.

"You'll have to catch up so we're all equally drunk." Cassidy laughed, clearly already a bit tipsy. Ian obliged, draining his glass and holding it out for a refill.

Clouds were gathering on the horizon, a welcome cool breeze pushing them rapidly overhead. As they ate and drank, they talked about the business. Kye was happy—connected in a way he wasn't used to. It wasn't just because of the way they'd included him with their stunningly generous offer of part of the business. Nor was it simply the sexual attraction that existed between them. It was more than that. The three of them seemed to connect on so many levels.

As he looked from one to the other, Kye considered which one he'd like to fuck right then, if given the chance. He actually couldn't decide. He'd already tasted the luscious sexual sweetness of Cassidy's beautiful body and knew he wanted more, much more.

Ian on the other hand, was an unknown. There had been a definite slow burn of desire building between them during the massage, but Kye wasn't yet sure how the confused relationship between Cassidy and Ian would affect any future exploration between Ian and himself. Again the possibility of a threesome entered his mind, traveling through his nerve endings and engorging his cock.

He finished his drink, enjoying the buzz produced by the alcohol. Cassidy refilled his glass and he didn't protest. They ate in silence for a while until one by one, they set their plates aside.

"That was delicious, as always, Kye." Cassidy rubbed her stomach in appreciation. "You've totally spoiled us."

"My pleasure." They were lying down in a row, Cassidy in the middle, her eyes closed. The clouds overhead were darkening and the air had the sudden heavy feel of impending rain, but none of them stirred. Kye touched Cassidy's arm, drawing his finger down toward her delicate wrist.

Ian turned on his side, his brown eyes fixed on Kye's face. Kye tried to read his expression. He could sense the confusion and perhaps some jealousy, but also the desire rising like a presence between them.

With a studied casualness, Ian brought his hand to rest on Cassidy's hip. Kye shifted so he too was on his side, Cassidy sandwiched between them. He let his own hand drop until it covered Ian's. They stared at one another. Kye's cock throbbed and he licked his lips in a slow, deliberate gesture. Ian's gaze didn't waver, nor did he pull away his hand. There was so much electricity between them the air was almost crackling.

Kye pulled back. "Lie on your stomach, Cassidy. We'll give you a massage." He glanced at Ian for confirmation. A massage would be a nice icebreaker for what Kye hoped would follow. Ian nodded, apparently game.

Kye tugged at Cassidy's T-shirt, lifting it so they could reach her bare back. He loved that she wasn't wearing a bra. He ran his fingers over her soft skin. Ian's hands joined his, pressing against the muscles in her lower back. Cassidy sighed contentedly and closed her eyes.

Kye felt a drop of water on his face and looked up. The clouds had darkened to gunmetal gray and looked swollen. There was a sharp crack of thunder and then all at once a heavy rain began to fall, drenching them in an instant. Jumping up, they scrambled to collect the dishes and glasses, abandoning the already-soaked blanket to its fate.

Hurrying inside, the three of them stood dripping on the kitchen floor. Ian grabbed several dishtowels from a drawer, which they used to towel their hair. Both Ian's and Kye's eyes were drawn to Cassidy's white T-shirt, soaking wet and completely see-through.

The thin cotton clung to her beautiful breasts, the tips of which poked hard against the fabric. Cassidy lowered her towel, no doubt aware of their eyes on her. She flushed and wrapped her arms around her torso as she shook back the wet hair from her face. Ian was riveted to the spot, his lips parted, his cock clearly outlined against his denim shorts.

Kye was aware of his own erection, which had flagged while they hurried out of the rain, but was again pulsing. "Come on. Let's go upstairs and get out of these wet things."

Chapter Six

Though they hadn't planned it, all three trooped into the master bedroom, which Cassidy had insisted Ian take when they'd first moved in. The master bath was much bigger than the small bathroom shared between the two other bedrooms where Cass and Kye slept.

Kye handed each of them a large bath towel. He stripped off his wet shirt and stepped out of his jeans without a trace of self-consciousness. Cassidy was wrapping the towel around her head.

"Take off that soaking shirt first." Kye's voice was commanding Cassidy's cheeks were pink, but she obeyed, removing the towel and letting it drop to the floor.

Ian caught his breath. His heart was beating too fast. He was dizzy and he knew it wasn't just from the rum. Why had he kept Cassidy at arm's length for so long? How could he have been so stupid, so shut down and self-centered to imagine things were better when kept on a superficial level? He wanted her more than he ever had.

Cassidy stood like a young goddess, her coppery hair falling in wet sheets past her shoulders, her perfect breasts tipped with dark pink nipples, distended and plump, ripe for sucking. She pulled off her shorts, leaving pink lacey panties that hugged the pooching lips of her sex. Ian groaned aloud with desire before he could stop himself. Cassidy flushed and bent to pick up the towel, this time wrapping it around her body.

Kye looked to him. "Take off those wet things. We'll all snuggle in that big bed of yours, if you're of a mind."

Now Ian focused on Kye—his eyes drawn to the thick, erect cock pointing upward at an angle toward his hip, barely covered by his black bikini briefs. He wanted Kye too, wanted him more than he'd ever wanted any other man.

He pulled off his wet clothing and left it where it fell, though he, too, kept on his underwear. In a daze of excitement, nerves and desire, he followed the pair into his bedroom. He watched as Cassidy dropped the towel and slipped beneath his sheets.

Kye stretched out beside her above the sheets, crossing his ankles and lacing his hands behind his head. Ian stood frozen at the end of the bed, trying to process what was happening— what he wanted to have happen. His body already knew, but his brain was taking a while to catch up.

"Join us?" Kye held out his hand in a welcoming gesture. "We'll just lie down like we were outside. No pressure."

Ian relaxed some at Kye's calm voice and easy tone. Kye was right—just lying down together, same as they had been on the picnic blanket, didn't mean they were signing up for anything.

Ian sat on the edge of the bed, hoping his voice didn't betray his nerves. "This feels strange," he admitted.

Cassidy nodded, though she remained mute, her large green eyes flitting from Kye to Ian.

Kye offered, "Aye, it's a new situation, but we don't have to define it. Just think of it as an adventure. A new adventure for all three of us. Let's give it a chance, why don't we?"

Cassidy reached out to Ian suddenly, her arms open in invitation, her expression pleading. Something snapped in Ian's heart—the dam he'd built to keep himself safe was washed away in a tumbling rush of desire and longing. Had she really wanted him all this time, as Kye had claimed? Could he have been so blind?

His heart tapping rapidly, he lay down beside Cassidy. Kye lifted himself on an elbow. "Now, I believe, before the storm interrupted us, we were about to give this lovely young woman a back massage. Is that your recollection, Ian?"

"Yeah." He smiled at Cassidy, who smiled shyly back.

Kye pressed her shoulder and Cassidy obeyed the unspoken directive, rolling over onto her stomach. He pulled the sheets down to her thighs, revealing her lovely, bare back and luscious ass. A thin line of pink silk spanned her hips, disappearing between her cheeks.

Kye began to massage Cassidy's shoulders. Ian sat up, kneading the soft flesh of her lower back. In a way, Ian felt as if he were back in high school, during those heady, experimental days when kisses were stolen and each touch was new and even terrifying. He could sense Cassidy's nervousness as well, though it was clear she wanted whatever was happening between the three of them. Only Kye seemed at ease—his touch confident, his expression calm.

Ian focused on Cassidy's body for a moment, moving his hands over the supple flesh, though he couldn't stop sneaking glances at the man across from him. Kye's body was muscular and lean, his cock jutting straight up on his belly, held in place by his underwear. The crown and at least two inches were exposed above the waistband.

Kye brought his hand to rest over Ian's and their eyes met. Ian wondered if Kye could hear the thud of his heart, or if Cassidy could feel it pulsing through his hands. Kye slid one finger upward along Ian's forearm. Tentatively Ian touched Kye's shoulder, hard muscle in rounded definition beneath his fingers. Cassidy lay still beneath them.

Kye smiled and shifted until he too was sitting up. Ian stared openly now at his body, fascinated by the fat head of the cock peeking out from his underwear. Cassidy's head was cradled in her arms, her face hidden. Ian pulled his gaze from Kye's cock, dropping his hand to cup one round globe of her lovely ass. She gave a small moan and arched up to meet his touch.

Kye, his eyes still on Ian's face, pushed his underwear down enough to reveal his shaft, which was thick and straight, engorged with blood. He gripped it and moved his hand up and down, the gesture deeply erotic. Ian was breathing too fast. He closed his mouth, willing himself to calm down.

His cock felt like it was going to explode. Following Kye's cue, he dared to grip his own shaft, though he didn't pull aside his underwear to do so, instead reaching into it. He closed his eyes a moment, savoring the pleasure and momentary relief his hand gave him.

He imagined Cassidy's mouth sliding hot and wet over it but the image shifted of its own accord to Kye kneeling before him, his dark head bowed as he took Ian's cock deep into his throat.

He opened his eyes to see Kye was still watching him, his gaze intense, almost fierce. Again he had the unsettling feeling of being utterly transparent, defenseless against Kye's discerning gaze.

Cassidy chose that moment to twist over onto her back. "What happened to my massage...?" Her words died in her throat and her eyes widened as she took in the two men, each with his hand wrapped around his cock.

"Oh." Her voice was soft and filled with wonder. Her tongue darted pink over her lower lip. Ian's cock ached for her mouth. His body tingled with the recollection of the smooth, silky perfection of her bare body and the gripping, wet warmth of her pussy.

74

Added to his desire for Cassidy was his undeniable lust for Kye. Kye had stretched out beside Cass, his hand resting on her hip. Again Cassidy held her arms out to Ian. He allowed her to draw him down. She wrapped her arms around his neck and pulled him close for a kiss.

As her lips sought his, she pressed the length of her body along his. She tasted of strawberries and rum. Her tongue moved eagerly in his mouth. Her erect nipples pressed against his chest, sending sparks of pleasure straight to his cock.

"Oh, Ian." Her voice caught in her throat, the longing in it making his heart wrench. He kissed her hard, hoping his kiss conveyed the words he didn't have. She kissed him back, her arms tight around him.

Ian reveled in the soft touch of her lips, but at the same time he was somewhat self-conscious, aware Kye was watching them. After several moments Cassidy pulled back and then snuggled against his chest, hiding her face.

Ian's eye was drawn to Kye's large hand, which had remained on Cassidy's hip. The hand began to move from her hip over the sensuous curve of her ass. Ian licked his lips as Kye hooked a finger beneath the waistband of her thong, dragging the fabric down until he'd pulled the panties completely from her body.

Cassidy had to be aware of what was happening, though her face remained hidden against Ian's chest. Was she okay with this? He pulled back from her and lifted her chin. Her cheeks were flushed, her eyes bright.

"You want this, Cass? You want us both?"

She nodded.

Kye stroked Cassidy's ass, his tan hand dark against her pale skin. Cassidy shivered and shifted so she was again lying flat on her stomach between the two men.

Kye placed a hand firmly on her thigh and nodded toward

Ian. Ian put his hand on the other thigh. As if they'd rehearsed it beforehand, they spread her legs apart. Cassidy's shoulders were rising and falling, her breath audible over the beating of the rain on the roof. Her face was obscured in a silky blanket of copper hair.

Their fingers slid toward each other over her slender thighs, focusing in on her center. Both men sat up, leaning forward to see her spread sex. Cassidy had a beautiful pussy—the labia like the petals of some rare, exquisite orchid.

Ian could hardly believe he was here with another man, with his best friend, Cass, spread bare before them. A sense of the surreal assailed him. He wondered briefly if he was drunker than he'd thought. Was whatever was happening right, or a huge mistake? Would this one afternoon of crazy risk result in his losing her forever?

He looked up sharply when Kye touched his arm. "It's okay." Kye's voice was barely a whisper. "She wants it. I want it. You want it."

Ian nodded. He did want it. Though he wasn't entirely sure yet what *it* was. He knew he wanted to have Cassidy back again as a lover. He wanted to fuck her, to feel her tight heat envelop him. He wanted to lick the moist, hot folds of her sex until her clit peeked at him from beneath its hood, and her desire seeped from her in a gush of lust.

What he wanted with Kye he wasn't prepared to fully articulate, not even to himself.

Kye drew a single finger along one side of her outer labia and Cassidy jerked but didn't close her legs. Feeling possessive, Ian moved his hand over her pussy, cupping it. Cassidy moaned and pushed against his fingers. Ian couldn't help but wonder if she knew whose hand it was. Did it matter?

He slipped a finger into her tight, wet tunnel. Cassidy wriggled back against him. The scent of her arousal was ripe in the room. Kye put his hand over Ian's, forcing Ian's finger deeper into Cassidy. She moaned again.

Ian moved his hand, rubbing in teasing swirls over Cassidy's labia, Kye's hand remaining on his. His cock was a steel rod. He glanced at Kye's cock, still bound in the low-riding underwear. "Take them off." He could hardly believe he'd spoken the words aloud.

Kye complied and his large, thick cock sprang free. He knelt up, taking his shaft in his hand, his gaze burning. Ian rubbed Cassidy's pussy, sliding a second finger in to join the first. Cassidy moaned, a shudder running sensuously through her body.

Ian was distracted from Kye's cock by her whimpers of pleasure. She began to tremble. Her labia were swelling against his hand. All at once the muscles of her sex clamped down on his fingers, her body stiffening and then convulsing in a series of orgasmic spasms.

Finally she collapsed limp against the bed, Ian's fingers still buried inside her. Carefully he withdrew them. Cassidy curled over onto her side. She was breathing hard and her fair skin was flushed pink. Her eyes were closed, her hair wild. Ian pushed the hair from her face, tucking what he could behind her ear.

"Lovely." Kye smiled, pointing to Ian's hand. His index and middle fingers were shiny with Cassidy's sweet nectar. Kye took Ian's hand and lifted it to his mouth.

Parting his lips, he sucked at Ian's fingers, his eyes burning into Ian's all the while. Ian found the gesture supremely erotic. He knelt up, using his free hand to stroke his cock.

"Let me." Kye knelt over the inert woman between them. Leaning forward, he pushed Ian's hand away. Gripping the base of Ian's shaft, Kye lowered himself until his mouth was a fraction of an inch from the head. Ian's cock throbbed in Kye's firm grip.

"May I?" Kye looked up at him.

"God, yes," Ian murmured, closing his eyes. Kye's mouth lowered over his shaft, wet heat enveloping him as Kye licked down toward his hand. Kye began to pump the lower half of the shaft while sucking and licking the sensitive head.

Ian opened his eyes to see Kye's dark head bobbing at his groin. He put his hands on Kye's shoulders for balance and surrendered himself to the exquisite pleasure. He was aware of Cassidy stirring beneath them, but was too intent on what was happening to pay much attention.

Soft hands were encircling his balls. Glancing down, he saw Cassidy below Kye. She had positioned herself so her head was beneath Kye's, her body stretched out perpendicular to theirs.

He closed his eyes again when her tongue darted out, licking his sac while fingers traced a line between his ass cheeks. All the while Kye continued to lick and pump his shaft. When he felt Cassidy's tongue gliding along the path of her fingers, its tip circling his asshole, he shuddered with pleasure, shifting on his knees to give her better access.

Cassidy licked at the puckered entrance, pressing the tip of her tongue past the circle of muscle. At the same time, Kye took him deeper, moving his hand so he could swallow the length of Ian's shaft. Ian groaned and bucked against them, no longer thinking who was with whom or what he wanted from it all.

He became sheer sensation, ecstasy bursting through his body, exploding in a shattering orgasm. He gripped Kye's shoulders to keep from falling as he spurted again and again down Kye's throat.

Finally he fell back and toppled to his side, his heart smashing against his ribs. Cassidy curled against him, nuzzling her face in his chest. Kye shook the dark hair from his eyes and sat back, wiping his mouth with the back of his hand. His cock still bobbed fully erect from his groin.

Ian smoothed Cassidy's hair, his focus on Kye's sexy body. Kye gripped his own shaft and began to stroke it, the heavy balls swaying beneath. Ian held his breath, riveted to the sexy scene.

He wanted to lick along the smooth, straight line of the shaft, tasting the salty musky sweetness of the man, but he didn't dare. Kye was watching him, his lips parted, fire in his eyes.

Cassidy rolled onto her back, her eyes following Ian's. "Oh." Her tone was part wonderment, part primal lust. She glanced back at Ian. "Let's help him, baby. Want to?"

Ian's heart began a slow, deep pound and his mouth watered in anticipation. He nodded. Together they rose onto their haunches and each pressed one of Kye's shoulders, pushing him down to the bed.

Cassidy put her hands on Kye's broad chest and began moving them down toward his groin. She glanced toward Ian with a question in her eyes. Ian had sucked cock in his life and had enjoyed it, but knew he wasn't ready for that yet with Kye— not with Cassidy watching him.

"You do it," he whispered.

Impulsively she leaned over Kye and kissed Ian's mouth. "I love you." She said it so quickly and quietly he wasn't entirely sure she'd said it at all. Before he could answer, she had pulled back, leaning down over Kye, her long hair sweeping his chest and stomach.

She sat up, lifting her hair, smoothing it back into a ponytail and tying it in a loose knot at the base of her neck. Several burnished strands immediately escaped, falling softly against her cheeks and neck.

Again she knelt over Kye, sliding her lips over the head of

his cock. She pulled up, running her tongue over the slit. Kye moaned. Though Ian had just climaxed, his cock twitched and swelled at the sight before him.

He glanced at Kye's face. His eyes were closed, dark lashes shadowing his cheeks. His lips were parted, his head back against the pillows. Ian stared in fascination as Cassidy took the shaft into her mouth until the full length of it was down her throat.

"Jesus, Mary and Joseph." Kye's voice was ragged.

Despite himself, Ian grinned, feeling a possessive pride in his girl's considerable skill. Cassidy lifted her head to draw a breath, pulling back enough so Ian could see Kye's cock, shiny and nearly purple with blood. After a moment she lowered her mouth, taking him deep.

Ian's cock was now erect again and he gripped it as he watched the erotic scene before him. He considered moving behind Cassidy and fucking her while she sucked another man's cock. The thought hardened his cock even more, but he made no move.

Kye was breathing hard, nearly panting. His fingers were entangled in Cassidy's hair, which had fallen completely out of its makeshift bun. He thrust his hips up to meet her mouth. Impulsively Ian rolled toward them, stretching his body out beside Kye's. He reached between them, finding and cupping one of Cass's perfect breasts. His fingers sought her nipple, which he squeezed and pulled, loving how it hardened to his touch.

Cassidy moaned around Kye's cock. Ian pressed his erection against Kye's hip, his hand still on Cassidy's breast. His heart was thumping against Kye's side. Kye turned his face toward Ian. Before Ian realized what was happening, Kye had pulled his head close.

He kissed Ian's mouth, the stubble of their beards brushing

as his tongue slipped between Ian's lips. Ian held himself still at first, caught off-guard. Somehow kissing was more intimate to him than oral sex. Yet he didn't pull away. Kye's kiss was sensual and intense, fueled no doubt by the hot mouth driving him to a frenzy at his groin.

Suddenly Kye twisted away with a cry. "Yes," he hissed, holding the word for several sibilant seconds as he shuddered against Cassidy. Ian moved back, fascinated as he watched Kye come. His eyes were squeezed shut, the tendons standing out on his neck, which was red with exertion.

Finally Cassidy released him, sitting back on her haunches, her eyes a luminous emerald green. Her cheeks and chest were flushed as if she'd just orgasmed herself. Her nipples were like dark pink gumdrops. Ian's cock jutted with appreciation toward her. He ached to take her in his arms.

Kye lay still between them, his eyes closed, a half smile on his face, the very picture of sexual satiation. He opened his eyes and lifted his arm on the pillow, inviting Cassidy to lie next to him. She sidled down beside him.

Ian lay on Kye's other side, not at all sure how he felt. Was what had just happened really about the three of them, or was it simply a way for Cassidy and Kye to have sex with his blessing? Not that they needed it, obviously. They'd made love before inviting him along for the ride.

Though he wished his mind would slow down, or better yet turn off, it refused. Thoughts swirled and eddied through his brain, as his old fears of mixing friendship and sex reared their twisted heads.

What would happen now? Was it only a matter of time before things fell apart? Would the carefully constructed relationship he'd rebuilt with Cassidy, after the nearly disastrous month as lovers, be destroyed by this whirlwind of sexual passion between the three of them?

I love you.

She *had* whispered that, hadn't she? And her saying it meant so much more than Kye's assurances that she was in love with him. But what would happen now? Was it possible to resume where they'd left off? Would he fall into his old patterns of finding his partner, or in this case partners, wanting, and break things off? As a result, would he now lose not only Cassidy, but Kye as well?

He glanced over at the two of them. They each had their eyes closed, each wearing a small, satisfied smile on their lips. *Why can't I be like that? Why can't I just live in the moment and take pleasure where it's offered?*

With a sigh, he too closed his eyes and let himself slip away.

Chapter Seven

Cassidy awoke with a smile on her face. She felt deliciously relaxed and very happy, though at first she couldn't recall the reason. She reached out, her hands encountering the smooth, soft sheets, but no sexy, warm male bodies.

The empty space beside her pulled her awake. The rain had stopped and the room was filled with purple and golden light from the setting sun. Both Kye and Ian were gone. Cassidy sat up and stretched, sleepily wondering where her two men had disappeared to.

Her two men.

Did she have the right to use that possessive pronoun? Was what had happened a result of the daiquiris or something more? Was it a one-time thing or the beginning of something real?

Kye was exciting and new, but her deep, abiding joy had been in tasting Ian's sweet lips again—in kissing and licking his hot, perfect body, in feeling his sexy tongue glide over her sweet spots. She shivered at the recollection, her hand dropping of its own accord between her legs. Slipping a finger into the wetness, she drew it up over her clit. She closed her eyes and sighed with pleasure.

I love you, she had admitted to Ian on an impulse. He hadn't answered in kind, not with words, but she'd felt his reaction as if he had. He loved her too—not just as a friend, but as more, she was sure of it.

And Kye, where did he fit in? Was he just a key, used to open Ian's heart and then be tossed away? Was it possible she was in love with him too? As her fingers swirled over her sex, the image of Kye, Ian's cock down his throat, loomed sensuously in her mind's eye.

One thing was for sure, those were the two sexiest men she'd ever been with, and they were gorgeous together, dark on blond, muscular, passionate and *hers.* "Yes," she whispered to the empty room, feeling their male heat around her as she rubbed herself. "I want them both."

She came with a gasp, her heart pumping in a pleasing thud. She lay still a while, recovering as the room darkened with the setting sun. Eventually she climbed out of the bed and padded to her own room to get dressed. She slipped on a fresh pair of panties and pulled on another sundress with spaghetti straps, the fabric a silky deep green. She stood in front of the mirror, shaking out her long wavy hair, which had dried while she slept. She pulled it back and tucked it behind her ears. It immediately and disobediently sprang back around her face. With a shrug, she turned away, eager to find the guys.

She skipped down the stairs on bare feet, surprised when she got to the bottom to find no one was there. "Ian?" she called out. "Kye?" She walked into the kitchen but it was empty, as was the rest of the downstairs. She opened the back door and peered out into the empty backyard. The wet blanket had been picked up from the grass and spread over a lawn chair to dry, but neither guy was in evidence. The car was still in the driveway.

Feeling an odd sensation, she retraced her steps to the second floor and moved past Ian's room and her own to Kye's room. The door was ajar, nearly closed. She heard muffled sounds within. Cautiously she pushed at the door, which opened silently.

The lights were off. The room was bathed in the blue wash of twilight. Kye stood by his bed, his hands on his hips, his head thrown back. Ian knelt in front of him, his blond head bobbing up and down at Kye's groin. Both men were naked.

They were in profile to the door, so Cassidy could see Ian's mouth lifting and lowering over Kye's thick, rigid shaft. He wasn't taking it all the way in, but focused mainly on the head, licking and sucking it like a lollipop. Kye moaned, dropping one hand to Ian's head, fingers gripping the short tufts of spiky blond hair.

Neither man appeared to be aware of her standing like a statue at the open door. Kye was panting—low, sensual moans punctuating the breathy gasps. He began to shudder and jerked forward, forcing the entire length of himself down Ian's throat. Ian reared back, gasping just as Kye's semen released itself in thick ribbons of pearly white that landed on Ian's face and broad, smooth chest.

Kye dropped down onto the bed, his chest heaving, still breathing hard. He leaned back, supporting himself with his hands. His dark hair had fallen into his face. He shook it back and sat up, touching Ian's shoulder.

After a few seconds or perhaps it was hours while Cassidy stood riveted to the spot, Kye spoke. "Sorry. That just kind of snuck up on me."

Ian was using a hand towel to wipe away Kye's ejaculate. "I never learned to swallow."

"Then we'll have to teach you," Kye answered with a grin.

Though Cassidy hadn't made a sound, Kye chose that moment to swivel his head toward the door. He locked eyes with her. A slow, easy smile moved over his mouth. "Ah. The sleeping beauty has awakened at last."

Heat blanketed her face, neck and chest. "I—I didn't mean to spy..." she stammered. It had been one of the sexiest scenes she'd ever witnessed, and yet she felt odd and disoriented, as if she'd been spying on strangers.

The sudden ghastly thought of the two men as lovers, lovers who didn't need a woman, didn't *want* a woman coming between them, struck her like a blow. Had her own greedy desire for them both blinded her to such a scenario? Was she so self-centered it had never even occurred to her they might prefer the company of one another to her?

Had Kye, instead of being a key to Ian's heart, been the key that would lock him away from her forever? Tears sprang to her eyes, though on some level she knew she was overreacting.

"Come here." Ian's voice was tender. Was it only pity? Had the real reason he'd insisted they return to being just friends been because he was gay? Had he only been waiting for the right *man* to come along? Was she merely the conduit he'd used to get what he really wanted?

Ian held out his arms to her. She wanted to move into them, but her feet wouldn't obey. She remained frozen where she stood.

"Cassidy, love. You look like you've seen a ghost." Kye patted the bed. "Come in here and sit down a moment. We didn't mean to carry on the party without you, but we didn't like to disturb you—you were sleeping like a baby."

"It's—it's okay," she lied. She knew she was being ridiculous. Why was she doing this? "I just—I just need a minute to collect myself, to, um, fix my hair."

She pulled at her thick tresses, aware she was babbling. "So I'll, um, see you later." She turned on her heel and raced down the hall to her room before she said anything even stupider.

"Shit." Ian stood, dropping the hand towel to the floor.

"She'll be okay." Kye tossed him his shorts and underwear,

which Ian pulled on hurriedly. "This is a lot to take in. Ménages can be kind of intense when the people involved care about each other. She was obviously at the door a while. It's got to be disconcerting to watch your lover with someone else, even if they have your blessing."

Ian had the suddenly unsettling realization he wasn't sure who Kye was referring to when he said lover. Who, in point of fact, did Cassidy regard as her lover? And who, then, was the third wheel in all this?

Yet he couldn't deny the afternoon had been amazing. He wasn't going to pretend the experience with Kye hadn't been incredibly hot. But he hated to see how upset Cassidy was. He had to do something, he had to fix it.

Kye, as usual, read his mind. "Go talk to her."

"I'm not sure what to say."

"Tell her the truth. The thing that matters most. Tell her you love her."

Ian knocked on her door. "Can I come in?" There was no answer. He turned the knob and opened the door. Cassidy was face down on her bed, her head hidden beneath her pillows.

He moved toward her and sat on the edge of the bed. "Cass." He touched her shoulder. She didn't move. "Hey, baby."

She rolled over. There were tears in her eyes but she smiled. "I'm sorry," she whispered. "I think it just took me by surprise, seeing the two of you like that. It was super hot but I was...jealous." She looked away.

"I'm sorry. Sorry I've been such a jerk for so long. I'm still not exactly sure what's going on, but whatever it is, I want you and me to be part of this equation." He stroked her hair, love surging through his heart, his defenses laid bare by the afternoon's passion, and even more by the tears in her eyes.

"Listen," he said earnestly. "You know me pretty well. Even so, I should warn you. I'm probably going to fuck this up. Not because I want to, but because I don't know how to act. I mean, you know firsthand how I can screw up a relationship."

Cassidy smiled and touched his arm. He put his hand over hers and squeezed. "I have to tell you, watching you and Kye these past weeks, and realizing what I was missing, what I was losing, what I had rejected because of my own stupid, fucked-up fears..." He shook his head, stunned at the enormity of what he'd been on the verge of losing, or more accurately, never allowing himself to find.

"I love you. I don't exactly know what else is going on. What you are to Kye or Kye to me or us to him. But when I can quiet the noise in my head, the one thing I know from the bottom of my heart is I love you. I don't want a life without you in it."

"Oh, Ian," Cassidy whispered. "I've wanted to hear those words from you forever." She held out her arms and he lay beside her, wrapping her tight. "I've tried so hard to be just friends, but I've never stopped wanting you. Not for one single second."

Ian's heart constricted with anguish. "But, Cassidy," he protested, "we had both agreed it was better—"

"It *was* better. I mean, when we were lovers things somehow just got more and more messed up. It was better to have you as a friend than lose you altogether."

"Cass, I'm sorry. I—"

"No, please." Cassidy put two fingers over his lips. "Don't apologize. That's not why I said it. I just wanted you to know— I've never stopped wanting you. I'm not sure what's going on with Kye either. He's a sexy, wonderful guy and this afternoon was incredible. I just want—I hope—that you and me, that we can have that closeness again without all the crap that went along with it. If I have to choose between having you only as a friend, or not having you at all, I'll take friends."

"I don't want you to have to choose—not ever again."

They held each other tight, silent for several minutes. Ian's heart felt so light he thought it might escape from his chest and rise to the ceiling. "Hey." He nestled his cheek against her soft hair and inhaled her wonderful scent. "You whispered something when the three of us were in the bed together. I couldn't quite hear it. Can you say it again?"

Cassidy pulled out of his arms and tilted her head with a smile. "I said I love you, Ian Tanner. I have, I think, since the moment I saw you at that pool party. I never stopped, not for one second."

"Me too," he answered, realizing it was true. "I was just too stupid to realize it."

"What about the *three* of us? What about Kye? I guess we better figure out what the hell we want, and let him know, huh? Judging on what I walked in on, you're not exactly impervious to his charms yourself." Playfully she punched him in the shoulder.

Ian was quiet a moment, trying to collect his thoughts. He did want Kye. Even in the face of their renewed commitment to each other, his cock rose at the memory of Kye and the afternoon's sexual adventure. Could two become three? Was such a thing possible?

"I guess I don't really know exactly what I want, do you? I know I'm into him. And it was incredibly hot being with the two of you. I have to say, I never really saw myself falling for another guy." He shook his head for emphasis. "But Kye McClellan... Well, I don't have to tell *you.*"

She nodded. "There's something about him. He's incredibly charismatic. Today was so hot. Even though I got kind of jealous watching the two of you, at the same time the rush was indescribable. I guess maybe we'd better talk to Kye and see where he fits into all this."

Kye's voice startled them both and they looked up to see him standing at the doorway. "Did I hear my name?"

"Aye, laddie," Cassidy answered in her attempt at a Scottish brogue. "That you did."

CX

Kye watched from the sidelines as the days unfolded, content to let the lovebirds reconnect. He was glad they were open to continuing the three-way, but recognized they needed a little space to discover each other again. One day became two and then three.

The three of them had talked candidly about what they wanted out of the newly formed ménage, at least as candidly as they could, given the fact none of the three was entirely sure. It was for that reason Kye had backed off, though he still wanted them both—very much.

Maybe, he thought with a twinge of sadness, he was destined to be on the sidelines, watching a core relationship develop, never really at its center. He knew this was a situation of his own making, but that didn't make him feel less lonely.

It had been hard these past few days, sometimes very hard, to know they were making love down the hall while he lay alone. Yet he'd sensed the timing wasn't right. He was a patient man, and as difficult as it was, he decided to wait.

Late at night, with only the crickets and cicadas outside his window for company, was when he thought most about Derek. Derek Simmons, the guy he'd followed to Texas, swept up in the misguided fantasy that they were in love, and love would conquer all.

They'd met on the Island of Crete at an outdoor café. Kye

had been sitting alone, enjoying the fresh fish chowder and crusty bread dipped in olive oil, along with a glass of strong, red, Greek wine. He was staring out at the incredibly blue water of the Mediterranean Sea, thinking about nothing in particular.

Derek had appeared before him, dressed in a cowboy hat and jeans, the telltale tourist's camera around his neck. "Excuse me." He spoke English, the accent pure Texan. "Do you speak English?"

Derek was tall and lean with a kind of coltish grace, all legs and collarbone. Kye invited him to sit down. Derek did so, taking off his hat to reveal a head of golden hair falling in long bangs over his forehead. His eyes were crystal blue, his mouth a feminine cupid's bow.

The chemistry between them had been instant. Derek was barely twenty-two, which should have been Kye's first clue to watch out. He was touring Europe for a few months, he told Kye, on his first trip outside of the U.S. on his own. "My graduation gift from college," he threw out in the offhand manner of the truly rich.

Derek ordered lunch and they began to talk about which Greek Islands each had visited and where they planned to go next. Kye couldn't seem to look away from Derek's eyes, as blue as the sea behind them. He kept losing the thread of their conversation as he tried to keep from drowning in those eyes.

Beneath the conversation something else was being communicated. Something primal, simmering and irresistible. Derek was staying in a private villa, much nicer than the hostel in which Kye had rented a room for the week.

He invited Kye in. "I'm a virgin." His cheeks turned pink. "With men." That was Kye's second big clue to turn and run, but he hadn't. His cock hardened at the idea of deflowering this innocent, beautiful boy.

He'd forced himself to go slow and easy, making sure Derek

was at ease every step of the way. Derek was a surprisingly passionate lover for one so young and inexperienced. The sex had been incredible. The outside world fell completely away as they focused on learning each other's bodies. Kye reveled in the taste of Derek's skin, the yielding sweetness of his virginal tunnel, their mingled sweat and rasping breath, the press of muscle and the beating of blood in their veins.

Kye moved into Derek's villa that night and they continued to travel together over the course of the next several weeks until it was time for Derek to return to Texas. "Come with me," he'd said impulsively, only two days before he was to depart. At the time, Kye had thought to return to Scotland for a while, though he had no firm plans.

Derek lived in a townhouse in the upscale neighborhood of River Oaks, Houston. He had only just moved out from his parents' house and was excited about living on his own, prepared to enter law school in the fall.

"This isn't the real world here in Greece, not for us," Kye had warned him. They were lying on soft pink sand, a cool sea breeze blowing over their bronzed bodies. "Your parents aren't going to like the idea of you bringing someone home. They think you're going to marry that Peggy Sue or whatever her name is."

"Brandy Sue," Derek had corrected with a laugh. Still, he'd admitted his parents had no idea he was gay, nor did Brandy Sue, who Derek said was saving herself sexually for marriage. He was engaged to be engaged—that was how he'd put it—to the daughter of another prominent Houston family. Kye could only imagine the fallout when he came back from Europe, "corrupted".

In fact there was no fallout because Derek hid the truth, and Kye. Kye wouldn't have minded not meeting Derek's family, but he didn't like Derek sneaking around and lying to his parents. Derek had insisted when back in Greece that he was going to stand up to his parents and his girlfriend and be true to himself. When he actually returned to the bosom of his family, that firm resolve melted away.

The days turned into weeks and still he hadn't come out. "They'd kill me," he finally admitted. "I just can't face it." Derek somehow thought he could keep Kye just waiting at home like a windup sex toy, and forget about him when he was gone.

The situation increasingly grated on Kye. Being in a new city with no ties and not even much of a music scene, Kye felt like a kept man, waiting at Derek's townhouse while Derek attended family functions and denied Kye's existence and his own newfound orientation.

While the sex was still phenomenal and his affection for Derek undisputed, he became less and less willing to remain hidden while Derek got his head together. Things came to a head when Derek told Kye over breakfast one morning that he and Brandy Sue had set the date.

Kye, who had so far kept his cool, trying to be patient while his young lover found himself, exploded in a fury of confusion and hurt. Throwing his things haphazardly into his duffel bag and grabbing his guitar, he headed for the door. Running after him, Derek hung onto him, pleading for him to stay.

"I love you," Derek cried, his voice cracking. "But you can't understand the pressure I'm under. My family goes back generations in this town. Houston may be a big city, but the mentality, at least in our crowd, is still very much small town Republican right-wing fundamentalist. If I admit I'm gay, my father will disown me so fast I won't even have time to pack. I'll be on the street."

"I understand," Kye said, though he didn't. He couldn't fathom choosing security and money over love. He focused on his anger, instead of his hurt, and shook Derek's hand away. "You won't have to worry about Kye McClellan. I won't darken your door again, I assure you."

Derek's voice was pleading. "I'm not like you. I can't travel around finding odd jobs. I want to be a lawyer. Eventually a judge. I want that big house and big car—you know, the American dream. You might say I'm selling out. But I'm a realist. Once I have my own career, my own life, things will be different. I still want to see you, Kye. I still love you and the sex is fucking amazing. But I can't keep hiding out like this. Brandy Sue is insisting on coming over—she wants to know why I've been keeping her away. My mom, too. She wants to see how the place looks since I had it decorated. If you could maybe just disappear for a few days. I'll put you in a nice hotel. Or maybe I could even get you an apartment or something. I have a pretty sizable monthly allowance."

Kye was rendered speechless. He didn't even try to explain the many different ways Derek had offended him to his core. "Good luck to you, Derek. I hope your chosen path makes you happy." He refused to look into those china blue eyes, now swimming with tears.

That morning Kye left. That night he met Cassidy. In the weeks he'd been living with Ian and Cassidy, he hadn't seen or heard from Derek, and he knew this was just as well. The stupid thing was, he still missed him.

Now he'd put himself in a kind of suspended animation, waiting to see how things shook out with Cassidy and Ian. He could have found comfort elsewhere. It was easy to pick up a man or a woman at one of the myriad clubs and bars in the city. He could have had a different partner every night of the week if he wanted.

The thing was, he didn't want that. Working and living with Cassidy and Ian had been fulfilling on so many levels. One of the reasons he'd left Scotland was because he'd been chafing under the tight yoke of control exercised by his father and his older brother when it came to running the family's business—a small but successful chain of departments stores in Edinburgh and Glasgow.

The business had been losing market share over the past several years, due, Kye was convinced, to their failure to upgrade their technology. Of the old school, Kye's father was suspicious of technology, computers and most definitely the Internet. Kye's brother, while not quite so out of touch, did whatever his father said, which frustrated Kye to no end.

With Ian Tanner Designs, while admittedly a much smaller operation, Kye had been given carte blanche to make the changes and upgrades necessary to successfully operate a small business. It was gratifying to see how well things were running in such a short time, and to know it was because of him. A share in the business had been a perk—he would have done it anyway.

Kye actually had a sizable bank account at his disposal, courtesy of his share in the family business. Occasionally he dipped into it, to pay for airline tickets and other large purchases, but when he could, he preferred to make it on his own, taking odd jobs and playing music gigs while he traveled.

Though he'd never mentioned it to Ian or Cassidy, when he first became involved in Ian Tanner Designs, he'd already decided to give it a cash infusion if the bank loan hadn't come through. For the first time in a long while, he actually was emotionally invested in something, something that mattered.

But more than the satisfaction of running the business, he loved the rich friendship blossoming between the three of them. He genuinely liked them both and felt completely accepted as one of the household. In a way, despite his nocturnal loneliness, he liked the fact they wanted him around and not just for sex. He liked cooking for them, pleased though somewhat amused at their continued awe over his ability to put real meals together. Apparently neither had taken the time to learn how to cook much more than scrambled eggs or hot dogs.

He had to be patient. They would come to him, in time. At

night when he was at his loneliest, he would remind himself of this and reassure himself he could wait one more day.

Chapter Eight

As orders continued to increase, they decided to hire a part-time assistant. Brenda came in three days a week and helped with the more mundane part of jewelry making, freeing Ian up for the design and the intricate work.

Kye had moved Cassidy out of the large downstairs studio to give Ian and his assistant more space. She was now installed in the sunroom off the kitchen, her photographic equipment, laptop and printer spread out on a large antique wooden table she had found at an estate sale. While Ian missed being able to look up and see her while he worked, the arrangement was definitely more productive for them both.

Using funds from their line of credit, Kye had purchased a second laptop, which he'd installed in the nook in the kitchen that held a small desk. On this computer Kye kept the books, ordered inventory, paid the bills, collected the accounts receivable and saw to it the business had enough cash to operate.

He relaxed by playing his guitar, sometimes just idly strumming while he hummed, other times completely engrossed in complex chord patterns and hauntingly beautiful melodies that invariably distracted Ian to the point where he had to stop what he was doing so he could listen. He felt almost guilty that they'd been the reason Kye had passed on the audition up in Austin. He clearly could have a career in music if he chose.

Selfishly, Ian was glad he had not chosen that path.

With Kye's expert help, the business was growing as fast as Ian could produce and Cassidy could get it photographed and posted on the website. Local business was booming as well. Ian realized with something approaching amazement that this little venture of theirs was actually going to make it.

It was wonderful to wake up with Cassidy beside him. What a fool he'd been to push her away. He wondered how long things would have stumbled along in limbo if Kye hadn't come onto the scene and shaken them both up—forcing them, especially himself, to realize what they were throwing away.

Kye had seemed intuitively to understand they needed some space. At first this suited Ian, focused on claiming the girl of his dreams. He couldn't get enough of her soft skin, her sweet kisses, her yielding body. She too seemed especially needy—not in a negative way, but as hungry for him as he was for her.

Now, though, as he became more secure in his relationship with Cass, Ian found himself wondering more and more about Kye. Would he be ready to resume where things had left off? Cassidy and he had stayed up late last night, discussing how they might approach him.

Ian admitted he was both eager and afraid. What if Cassidy decided she preferred Kye to him? What if the thrill of three eventually wore off, and she chose the other man? How could he blame her, after all? His track record had been pretty lousy so far—why should she trust that things had changed?

In his heart, he knew they had. Something hard and bitter that had been lodged there—perhaps spawned by his parents' loveless relationship, and nurtured by his own fear of intimacy and inability to connect—had somehow melted away when the three of them had come together. It was as if Kye were the missing cog—what Ian had needed. He had forced Ian to face the truth of his real feelings for Cassidy, and also of his

98

homoerotic desires.

He had no idea if a ménage à trois could actually evolve into something meaningful and long term. Nor did he know if he yet possessed the emotional maturity and courage to work through whatever jealousies might again weave themselves into his psyche. But he wanted to try. He wanted to find out, and he wanted to do it with Cassidy at his side.

Kye, introduced to Mexican food their first night together, had fallen in love with the rich, spicy dishes. He had recently bought a Mexican cookbook and Ian and Cassidy were the lucky recipients of his efforts. That night over chicken enchiladas verdes, they sat around the kitchen table and talked about nothing in particular, enjoying the spicy food, complemented by cold beer they drank from sweating bottles.

That morning Cassidy and he had agreed it was definitely time to bring up the idea of resuming their sexual explorations with Kye. Cassidy had asked Ian to be the one to bring it up. Feeling a little shy, he finally found a segue when Kye raised his beer bottle in the manner of a toast and offered, "To success. To friendship. To the three of us."

They clinked their bottles. Ian figured it was as good an entry as any. "The three of us," he echoed. Nervously he licked his lips and plunged on. "We were thinking, Kye. If you were still interested—"

"Because *we* are, *very*," Cassidy interjected. Ian smiled at her eagerness. The smile broadened to a grin as she blushed and looked down.

He continued. "I know we've been kind of cocooning for a while. But we really miss you. We miss what was starting to happen between the three of us. We wondered if you were, um, maybe interested in reopening that particular door..." Aware he was himself now blushing, he tried to be more direct. "We want to have a ménage. You know. A threesome. If you were still inclined, that is."

Kye's clear gray eyes darkened as he swept them both with an enigmatic gaze. Ian held his breath. A smile curled over Kye's sensual, full lips. Cassidy was watching Kye, her eyes bright, her lips parted.

"I thought," Kye said finally, his smile erupting into a grin, "you'd never ask."

Kye surveyed the handsome young couple beaming nervously but expectantly at him from across the table and he had to laugh. His cock hardened at the thought of having the two of them naked and willing, even eager, to be with him.

Ian jumped up from the table. "Let's have some of that Port that Cassidy bought the other day." He moved toward the wine rack and selected a bottle, returning to the table with it and three small glasses. He started to uncork the bottle.

Kye pushed back from the table and stood. "I have a better idea. Let's have it upstairs."

They settled on the bed in the master bedroom, each holding a small glass of the strong, sweet wine. Kye could tell they were both nervous. Truth to tell, he was a little nervous himself.

Cassidy drank her wine quickly and poured herself a second. *Courage in a bottle*, Kye grinned to himself. She reached into the drawer of the nightstand beside the bed and pulled out a deck of cards.

"I have an idea." She giggled. "Let's play strip poker."

"You're terrible at poker." Ian laughed.

"That's the idea," she retorted with a grin.

Ian dealt the cards and they played a few rounds. None of them was wearing that much to begin with. Kye and Ian lost their shirts. As predicted, Cassidy was stripped to only her underwear in short order.

Kye found it difficult to concentrate with Cassidy's lush, round breasts bared in front of him. Ian, too, kept casting glances her way. Ian lost his shorts next. His erection was boldly outlined in his underwear, matching Kye's own, still hidden beneath his shorts.

Cassidy lost the last hand. Ian and Kye watched as she slid the silky panties down her slender thighs. Kye's gut tugged with desire. He ached to feel her sweet, tight heat envelop him once again.

With a coyness Kye found charming, Cassidy hid her face with her hands and lay down between them. Ian brushed the cards into a pile while Kye stretched out beside the beautiful girl.

"No fair." Cassidy peeked between her fingers. "You both have to get naked too."

Kye didn't need to be told twice. He pulled his shorts and underwear off and tossed them to the floor. Ian also stripped and in a moment they were all naked, thighs touching thighs. Kye turned in toward Cassidy, his cock pressing hard against her hip.

Ian turned inward as well, reaching over Cassidy to touch Kye's shoulder, feeling suddenly shy. "Here we are again."

Kye smiled. "Aye, that we are. And it was worth the wait, I assure you." He stroked one of Cassidy's creamy, soft breasts, his fingers moving toward the stiffening nub at its center. Ian leaned down, taking the other nipple between his lips.

Cassidy moaned, arching up to meet their touch. Kye slipped a hand down, finding the wet cleft between her legs, drawing another moan from the girl.

He looked at Ian, who was watching him intently, his expression hard to read. "I want you," Kye mouthed silently. Ian nodded, his eyes hooding. They leaned toward one another over Cassidy, their lips meeting in a closed-mouth kiss.

After a moment Ian parted his lips. Kye slipped his tongue between them, sliding it along the gum line above his top teeth, tasting the wine. Ian shivered, slipping his own tongue into Kye's mouth. While they kissed, Kye's fingers remained at Cassidy's pussy, slipping into her wetness and feeling the tight clamp of muscle.

Ian reached blindly over her, seeking Kye's cock. Kye rolled back to give him better access, still keeping a finger buried in Cassidy's tunnel. Finally Kye pulled back from Ian's kiss, though Ian's hand remained firmly wrapped about his cock. He withdrew from Cassidy's pussy, sliding his hand over her distended clit.

Cassidy gave a low, throaty moan. "What do you want, Cassidy?" Kye teased. "Use your words."

"Y'all," she whispered. "I want both of y'all."

Kye met Ian's eye and grinned back. "You heard the lady. She wants us both. Have you, uh, got something handy there?"

Recognition dawned in Ian's face and he twisted toward the nightstand, from which he withdrew two condoms. He tossed one to Kye and tore off the wrapper of the second one. As Kye rolled the condom onto his shaft, he noticed Ian removing the tube of lube and wondered just who was going to be fucked by whom and how.

Ian stretched out beside Cassidy. "What if *we* both want *you?*" he teased. "At the same time?"

Cassidy's cheeks flushed dark pink. Her nipples were even darker, erect and enticing. She sat up, looking from one to the other. "I've always fantasized about two guys at once."

Cassidy knew she was blushing, but she didn't care. She wanted this too much to censor herself. She hadn't been lying— the idea of double penetration with two of the sexiest men on the planet left her soaking wet.

She had had some experience with anal sex and she liked it, once she relaxed enough to fully accommodate a cock in her ass. But could she handle it with another cock in her pussy?

Both men were watching her. Kye tilted his head, appraising her. "I take it from your remark you've never had two guys at once?"

"No," she whispered, her heart thumping.

Kye turned toward Ian. "What about you? Does this sound like something you'd be into?"

"Sure." Ian's cock, bobbing and fully erect, seconded the motion. "Absolutely."

Cassidy looked at Ian helplessly, not sure what to do next. Fortunately, he made the decision for her. Lying down on his back, he reached for her.

"Come here, sweetheart. Straddle me. I'm desperate for you."

Eagerly Cassidy positioned herself over his cock, aware of Kye's penetrating gaze upon her. Carefully she lowered herself onto Ian's cock, unable to stifle the moan of pleasure as he filled her. She rode him for a minute or so, savoring his full hardness inside her.

Kye moved behind her until he was crouching on his knees. He pressed on her back, forcing her forward so her ass was angled toward him, the cheeks splayed by her position.

Though incredibly turned on, Cassidy was glad she could hide her face against Ian's chest. There was the sudden jolt of something cold against her sphincter. In a fraction of a second she figured out it must be the lubricating jelly.

Kye's finger swiveled around her nether entrance and eased its way inside, moving in a swirling motion that felt good. At the same time, Ian gave her a long, lingering kiss that distracted her for a moment from Kye's attentions.

She began to move again against Ian's cock, Kye's finger still lodged in her ass. After a moment he withdrew it and she could hear him positioning himself behind her. She stiffened, suddenly anxious. She wanted this, yes, but she was still nervous. Could she handle Kye's thick cock back there? What if he hurt her and she made a fool of herself? Despite her best intentions, Cassidy tensed. This wasn't going to work!

Nervously she turned back toward Kye. "I'm not sure..." she began.

"Shh," Kye soothed. "Nothing happens until you *are* sure, lass. That's a promise now and always. Relax. We go at your pace."

She nodded, believing him. She relaxed when instead of the press of the fat cock head, he inserted two fingers into her ass, moving in a gentle rhythm. Ian continued to move beneath her, his cock buried deep.

After a few moments, Kye leaned over her and whispered, "You're doing beautifully, sexy girl. I'm going to add another finger just to help you relax. You're so tight, so good. Hmmm, I can't wait to fuck you."

Her ass was well-lubed now and opening to Kye's persistent though gentle touch. Still, when the head of his cock touched her nether hole, she jerked forward, stifling a small gasp.

"Hey, it's okay, baby," Ian whispered, reaching up to push her hair from her face. "Kye knows what he's doing. Relax."

"Aye, I won't hurt you. We'll go slow and easy. We've got all night." Kye stroked her back. A warmth rose through her and she was finally able to fully relax, though her pussy throbbed.

She began to move again, sliding back and forth on Ian's iron rod. Each time she pushed back, the head of Kye's cock pressed against her ass. His hands rested just below Ian's as he began to guide himself inside her. Cassidy tensed again, squeezing her eyes shut as she waited for the sharp pain of initial penetration. There was no pain, however. Only the incredible fullness of Ian's cock deep inside her, joined by Kye's slow easing in from behind.

Cassidy wondered again for a panicked moment if she could handle it. Then Kye began to move and all fears flew out of her head. The sensation was indescribable. She could feel them both at once, creating an amazing friction. It was almost as if one huge cock were inside her, filling her from the inside out.

She began to shudder against Ian's cock as Kye moved in and out, still careful, but now fully inside her.

"Jesus," Ian moaned. "I can feel it too. It's incredible." He began to thrust his hips upward to meet her. The friction on her clit against his pubic bone was intensified by his motion. Kye moved faster behind her, his cock sending spirals of pleasure through her body that met and collided with the ecstasy caused by Ian's shaft buried deep in her pussy.

What are you doing to me? What are you both doing to me? This is amazing. This is so fucking intense. Jesus, don't stop, don't stop. Don't ever stop. Oh. My. God. I'm going to come... That's what Cassidy wanted to say, but each thrust from below and behind rendered her speechless. All that came from her lips was, "Wh...wha...wha..."

Finally she gave up all pretense of coherence, her voice rising in a sharp keen she could no more control than the writhing spasms of her body as she was hurtled into the most powerful orgasm of her life.

Somewhere from the height of her passion she was dimly aware of the men coming as well. Ian slipped over the edge first, bucking hard against her, only adding to the intensity of her own climax. A few seconds later Kye groaned, slamming even deeper into her. She was completely open to him though, and felt no pain from the onslaught.

Wantonly she pressed herself back against his shaft, eager to take him to the hilt. He fell forward over her and she collapsed beneath him, Ian's cock still buried inside her pussy.

It was as if her body had turned to lead. She literally could not move. Not only was she pinned beneath Kye, but her muscles refused to cooperate. She tried and failed to lift her hand. Kye's heart was tapping a rapid tattoo against her back. Ian's chest was slick with sweat against her breasts.

"You okay?" he murmured.

"Mmph," she managed, hoping this would be interpreted as, "Yes, but please get Kye off me, I can't breathe."

Miraculously, her silent wish was granted. Kye rolled from her, his spent cock sliding from her ass. Ian shifted, depositing her onto her back between them. He leaned over her, pushing her heavy hair from her face, for which she was grateful.

They all lay silently for a while. Eventually the pattering thud of her heart eased and this time when she tried, she was able to raise her hand and curl it into a fist, though even that small gesture was exhausting in her present state of sexual languor. She dropped her hand to her side and sighed.

She turned to look first at Ian, then at Kye. Both men were lying on their backs, their eyes closed, a satisfied smile on each handsome face. Perhaps feeling her eyes on him, Kye opened his and turned to face her.

"So, Cassidy. What's the verdict? Is DP for you?"

"You know," she pretended to ponder. "I'm just not sure yet. Maybe we should try it again?"

CB

Cassidy was vaguely aware of the sound of deep male voices swirling just outside her consciousness. She was skimming along sweet dreams, the three of them lying on white warm sand, aquamarine waves crested in white breaking near their feet.

After the amazing sex, they'd lain together, touching each other, kissing and fondling, intermittently dozing. Cassidy had only been half-kidding when she said she wanted to try it again, but she was content to lie between them, feeling their strong, masculine hands moving over her body, and running her own hands over their muscular, beautiful forms.

She hadn't been aware she'd fallen asleep until she awoke, finding herself alone. Through the window she could see fat, round clouds that appeared to be lit from within by pink candlelight. She heard the sound of the shower running.

Entering the bathroom, she could make out the shapes of two men in the glazed glass of the shower door. At once her pussy perked up, moistening in anticipation. "Hey, is there room for three in there?"

The shower door opened and Kye stuck out his head. "Cassidy, love, come join us. You were sleeping so soundly we hated to wake you."

She stepped into the steamy spray. The men positioned her between them, giving her a chance to get properly wet. Kye began to wash her hair, while Ian soaped her body with his strong, sexy hands. Kye stepped aside as Ian moved behind her, his hands lingering over her breasts, cupping and lifting them as he nuzzled her neck beneath the hot spray of water. She closed her eyes, surrendering herself to the heavenly attention.

After a while, she leaned back her head, rinsing her hair. The little stall was filled with steam, though the water was turning from hot to tepid. Ian shut it off but none of them moved to step out. Both men were watching her with hungry eyes.

Cassidy lifted and coiled her hair, squeezing out the excess water. She glanced down at their sleek, wet bodies, licking her lips at the sight of their cocks, both erect and waving toward her.

Without a word, she knelt between the two men so her face was level with their groins. She wrapped her fingers around Ian's shaft with one hand, while turning her head to lick the crown of Kye's erect cock. Kye moaned his approval. Lowering her mouth over him, she suckled and licked him.

She loved the feel his hard member filling her mouth and throat, cutting off her breath, though it was at her choice. She milked his cock with her tongue and throat muscles, thrilling to his sensual moans and sighs of pleasure. It wasn't long before he came. Eagerly she swallowed his offering.

Next she turned her attention to Ian, whose cock was as hard or harder than Kye's. She loved the taste of him, pungent and spicy, at once familiar and new. Ian cupped her cheeks with his hands as she suckled him, thrusting deep into her throat. She craved the delicious feeling of both surrender and control sucking a man's cock gave her.

All too quickly she felt the familiar, lovely tremor surge through Ian's body as he prepared to climax. She increased the tempo and pressure until he gasped, holding her head still as he thrust deep into her throat, nearly gagging her as he came.

He let her go and looked down at her, tenderly tucking her wet hair behind her ears in a sweetly intimate gesture that brought a smile to her lips. He held out his hands and she took them, allowing him to pull her to her feet. Ian wrapped her in his arms, whispering into her ear, "That was so hot, baby. I love you."

As they dried themselves Kye suggested, "It's Sunday. Let's take the whole day off—you too, Ian. Not a lick of work, promise? After breakfast, we'll spend the day in bed. Sound good?"

Cassidy and Ian looked from Kye to one another and said in unison, "Sounds great."

Chapter Nine

After a breakfast of pancakes, bacon, fresh orange juice and coffee, the three lovers returned upstairs to continue where they'd left off. During the meal, they talked in general about what they were going to do, Kye wanting to be sure everyone was comfortable with the plans.

Both Cassidy and Ian had agreed the idea was hot, but Ian was nervous nonetheless. Though he'd done just about everything else with a guy, he'd never actually had anal intercourse. He enjoyed the sensation of something up his ass, like a small dildo or a finger, but that's as far as it had gone.

"No pressure," Kye assured him. "We go only as far as you want to go. Only as far as feels good and right for all three of us."

They romped for a while in the sheets, kissing, touching, licking and holding. At one point Ian found himself beside Kye, both of them with their heads near Cassidy's hot, sweet pussy. Without discussing it, they both moved closer, pressing her thighs apart. Taking turns, they lapped at her fragrant, slick labia. Ian's cock stiffened with each breathy cry of pleasure.

While he was taking a turn licking his lover into ecstasy, Kye's lips closed over the head of Ian's shaft. Ian moaned against Cassidy's pussy. Each lick of Kye's tongue drove him to lap faster. Cass's clit was swollen and within minutes she began to shudder and pant, coming hard against him.

He held her, his tongue continuing to tease her until she pushed him away with such force he knew she meant it. With a grin, he lifted his head and wiped his mouth. Kye let Ian's hard shaft slip from his mouth.

While Cassidy lay there recovering, Kye murmured, "You ready, Ian?" He tossed Ian a condom. Silently they rolled the sheaths over their cocks.

Ian stared at Kye's endowment and bit his lip. Reading his mind, Kye said soothingly, "Only when and if you want it. Not a second before."

Ian nodded. He turned his attention toward Cassidy, who lay limp as a rag doll, a half smile on her pretty face, her eyes closed. He flipped her over. Pulling her ass up toward his groin, he positioned himself behind her.

"I need to fuck you," he whispered into her ear. Cassidy responded with a moan, wriggling back toward him. He positioned his cock at her wet entrance, reveling in its satin heat as he sank into her.

He draped himself over her back, supporting his weight on his hands so he wouldn't crush her. He began a slow pelvic thrust, sliding deep inside her and then pulling nearly but not all the way out.

He both heard and felt Kye behind him. There was a cold dollop of lube on his asshole. A moment later he felt what must be Kye's finger, just a single finger, running its tip along the rim. It felt good and when Kye pressed into the nether entrance, Ian pushed back to receive him.

His cock was enveloped in Cassidy's velvety warmth. He kissed her back while he fucked her, his attention split between the tight grip of her pussy and the newly added second finger in his ass.

Kye pressed the two fingers deeper. "It's so hot," he murmured. "That's it, Ian. Open yourself to me. That's it..." Kye

Claire Thompson

withdrew his fingers. Ian grunted when a third finger, slick with lube, joined the other two. It didn't hurt—it just felt very full.

"Perfect," Kye encouraged. "You're nearly ready for me, Ian. If you want me inside you, your body is relaxed now to take me without any pain." As he spoke, he reached beneath Ian and cupped his balls in his hand. The sensation, coupled with the aching pleasure of Cassidy's cunt and Kye's fingers still buried in his ass nearly made Ian come then and there.

"Yes," he managed to pant, forcing himself to hold on. "Yes, I want it. Do it. Fuck me. Fuck me."

The fingers were withdrawn. A moment later the tip of Kye's cock touched his virgin orifice. He tensed and Kye stilled at once. "I'm not going to move. You move back against me, Ian. Take your time. We'll stop if you need to."

Ian didn't want to stop. Though he was deliciously distracted by Cassidy's hot pussy massaging his cock and her beautiful ass slapping back against him, he ached to feel Kye's cock inside him.

"No. I want it," he said fervently.

"Okay. You dictate the pace. Push back, and stay relaxed."

Thoroughly lubed and in a heightened state of arousal, Ian pushed back against the fat head of Kye's erect cock. There was a moment, not so much of pain, but of resistance, as the crown was forced past the sphincter. Ian jerked forward and Kye's cock popped out.

He moved back again. Kye held his shaft, making it easier for Ian to press back against it. This time the head slipped in easily. It felt good. Better than good.

"Yes," Kye crooned. "Move back again. More. Don't stop this time. You can do it."

Ian obeyed, pressing back against Kye's cock. Kye gripped his hips and moved forward, this time not stopping until he was buried to the hilt in Ian's ass.

112

"God," Ian moaned.

"You did it," Kye's voice was throaty.

The feeling was like nothing he'd ever experienced. Awareness that he was being fucked by a man both excited and shocked him. At the same time, he experienced a surge of power as he thrust into Cassidy's tight, perfect heat.

Kye began to move inside of him. Cassidy pushed back just as Kye was pushing forward. Ian was enveloped in sensation, awash in delirious pleasure. He continued to move inside Cassidy, while Kye swiveled behind him, matching his intensity and thrust. Cassidy's feminine cries were punctuated by Ian's grunts and Kye's groans. The room was redolent with the scent of pure lust.

Ian slowed, not wanting to come too soon. He wanted this amazing pleasure to last as long as possible. Reaching around Cassidy, he sought her clit. Using three fingers pressed together like a Boy Scout's salute, he rubbed over her sensitive spot, causing her to gasp with pleasure.

"Ian," she murmured. "Yes, yes. Don't stop. It's perfect. Yes..." Her body began its orgasmic shudder, her vaginal muscles clamping down on his shaft, sending spirals of ecstasy hurtling through his loins.

Kye thrust hard behind him, forcing a grunt from his lips, and causing him to slam against Cassidy, who was crying out now as she orgasmed. She would have fallen forward, but he held her in place, reveling in the tight, trembling embrace of her cunt.

Unable to hang on a second longer, he let himself go. He came harder than he ever remembered coming in his life, Kye's thick cock still buried deep inside him. He started to fall against Cassidy, but Kye's strong hands held him up long enough to complete his own thrusting release.

Then they tumbled forward, Kye dragging him to the side

as he fell. They lay as they landed, Ian sandwiched between his lovers, his cock still inside Cassidy, Kye's cock still inside him.

Hearts thumped, sweat cooled, breathing slowed. When he found the strength to speak, Ian wondered aloud, "How in hell are we ever going to top this?"

"Lad." Kye laughed. "We've only just begun."

℃⅔

Days melted into weeks as May faded into June. The wheezy central air conditioning system could barely handle the hot humid days and sticky, only slightly cooler nights of a Houston summer in full force.

The three lovers continued their erotic exploration. Kye often fell asleep in the bed with Ian and Cassidy after an extended session of lovemaking and play. Other times he would return to his own room, craving the solitude of a man used to being on his own.

It wasn't that he didn't like being with them or being an integral part of their lives. He still enjoyed the day-to-day running of the business and loved the nighttime sexy romps. He especially loved watching Ian flower sexually as he grew more comfortable both with sharing Cassidy and exploring his homoerotic desires.

Cassidy, too, was blossoming into a confident, sensual woman. As time passed and Ian didn't pull back from her emotionally, she became surer of herself. Gone was the restless, sexually hungry but insecure girl he'd met at the bar. She was more like a sleek cat now, purring her sexual contentment when she lay sated between her two men.

Sometimes Kye found himself wondering what he himself wanted out of the relationship. After all, how long could it last?

He wasn't the sort of man to settle down—at least he never had been in the past. And while he still found the jewelry business to be rewarding and challenging, and still loved having sex with the eager, sensual couple, he knew in his heart it was only a matter of time before his gypsy blood got the better of him, and he packed his meager belongings and made his escape.

One night he slipped away from the master bedroom, carefully disentangling himself from his sleeping lovers' arms. He needed some time to himself. He lay down in the single bed in the room he'd never really made his own and stared out the window at the halo of the street lamp.

Unbidden, Derek slipped into his mind. Not the pleading, tearful Derek he had last seen, but the eager, passionate young man in Greece—lusting for sexual knowledge and ready to try anything. He could picture Derek lying beside him on the beach, his sun-kissed blond hair falling in his face, his body a study in masculine perfection. He saw those clear blue eyes opening, a smile curling his lips as he focused on Kye beside him.

"I want you," Derek would say. It was all he had to say. Though it was only the end of March, the weather had been unusually cooperative, providing them with an Indian summer of perfect, sunny days and cool nights. They would roll their towels and walk back toward his villa, spending the better part of each afternoon exploring every nook and cranny of each other's bodies with fingers, lips, tongues and cocks until they collapsed from sheer exhaustion.

The change that came over Derek began as early as the flight back to the States. It was subtle at first—holding his body a little apart from Kye's, where in Greece he was always touching him in some way—a knee beneath the table, a hand over his, even just shoulders touching as they sat side by side staring out at the wide blue expanse of the Mediterranean Sea.

Closing his eyes, Kye could still see the tops of the red-tiled roofs of the villas spreading out below them. He could almost taste the strong, flavorful coffee and the delicious sweet cheese pastries, still warm from the nearby bakery. He could see Derek, his blue eyes, his red lips, his hard, thick cock...

What a change once they were in Houston. Derek's emotional withdrawal, instead of easing as time passed, grew more and more pronounced, eventually leaving nothing but the sex between them, and even that, it turned out, was for Derek a shameful secret.

Kye examined his memories like a finger probing a wound. It hurt, but not as much as it once had. He was pretty much over Derek. After all, they'd never been in love. He knew that now. It was sexual infatuation, pure and simple. In fact, they didn't even have much in common, besides sex.

Derek had done so little with his life. It wasn't that he was boring or stupid, he was just young. His frame of reference was still so narrow, and he'd been spoiled and sheltered all his life. Kye was better off without the conflicted, immature Derek.

He was happy right now with Ian and Cassidy, but he couldn't help but wonder sometimes where it was all going. Would he ever be able to get past the small but persistent feeling of being a novelty, one that would eventually wear thin? After all, Cassidy and Ian had been together for a couple of years before he entered the scene, even if most of that time was spent as friends.

He shook his head, thinking how the term covered so much or so little when it came to the two of them. It was amazing to him that Cassidy had been willing to settle for a return to their platonic relationship, just to be near the man she secretly loved. Would he have been able to sustain that kind of relationship, keeping his innermost desires locked away? Would he have wanted to?

And Ian, his own feelings also under lock and key, even from himself, hidden by his fear of getting too close. What had happened in his life to leave him so defended? He seemed so open now, so obviously and completely in love with Cassidy. Had it taken another man making love to her under his roof to finally open his eyes and his heart?

And what of himself? As close as he felt to them both, could he ever compete with their history, with their level of connection? As wonderful as things were now between them, as friends, lovers and partners, he couldn't help but ask himself again how long it could last. More to the point, how long did he want it to last?

Kye was startled from his reverie by the ringing of his cell phone. He grabbed the phone, his mind at once veering to some kind of family emergency in Scotland. Without taking the time to see who it was, he flipped open the phone. "Kye McClellan."

"Kye. I did something really stupid." The words were slurred and muffled. Kye wasn't even sure he'd heard them right.

"What? Who is this?"

"Kye. Where are you? Are you still in Houston?"

Kye sat up abruptly, his heart thudding.

Derek.

"Yeah. What the hell's going on? You sound panicked."

"Thank God you're still in town. I didn't know if you would be. I have no one else to turn to. I'm in trouble. I got mugged. Worse." A pause, then a slurred, cracking voice. "I'm such a fuck up."

Kye's stomach flipped with apprehension. "What happened? Are you hurt? Where are you? Did you call 911?"

"In my car. No, I didn't call anyone but you. I'm okay. I mean, nothing's broken. I did something really stupid—" He cut himself off and took a deep, shuddering breath.

"Where are you? Are you drunk? Can you drive?" Kye was

up, pulling on jeans with one hand, his phone still to his ear.

"Yeah, drunk. How can you tell?" Derek laughed weakly. "I can drive, but I don't have my keys. I lost them when they— Jesus, I can't tell you. I'm so embarrassed. I had no one else to call."

"I don't get it. You said you didn't have your keys, but you're in your car? You left the doors unlocked?"

"No. I have that combination lock thing on my door, so I can get in without a key. Quit with the third degree, will ya? This neighborhood's really bad. Just come get me. Please?"

"Yeah, okay."

Kye pulled on a T-shirt and hurried down the hall. He glanced in at the sleeping pair, wondering if he should wake them or just leave a note. He decided on the latter. With any luck, he'd be back home before they even knew he'd been gone.

He raced down the stairs, the phone still to his ear. "I'll be there as soon as I can. Hang on a sec." Using the message pad beside the kitchen phone, he scrawled a note that he'd gone to give a friend whose car was broken down a lift and he'd be back shortly.

Grabbing the keys from the hook beside the front door, he hurried toward Cassidy's car. The phone still to his ear, he demanded, "Tell me exactly where you are."

"I'm near the ship channel. The street signs say Lyon Avenue and McKee. I'm near a bar called The Cesspool. These two guys...I can't tell you. I'm so embarrassed."

Kye's stomach twisted again. "Did they hurt you, Derek?"

"Not fatally." Derek barked a mirthless laugh. "It's a gay bar. A dive. When I got there I knew I shouldn't even walk in, but I'd heard it was a hot scene, and it's nowhere I'd ever run into anyone I know, that's for sure. I had fun at first. But then I met these two guys. Fred and Victor. They took me back in an alley behind the bar. Oh God, I can't—" His voice choked off in a sob.

"Derek, it's okay. We'll talk about it later. For now just sit tight and make sure your doors are locked. I'll be there as soon as I can. I'm going to hang up now so I can concentrate on getting there."

Not being familiar with the city, except for Montrose and River Oaks, he stopped at a gas station and bought a map. As he paid for it, he asked the clerk behind the counter, "Could you tell me how to get to the ship channel? To Lyon Avenue and McKee?"

The man, a short, stocky guy with a shaved head and a weary expression, shook his head. "The ship channel? What the hell you want to go there for in the middle of the night? Get yourself killed, like as not."

"A friend's car is broken down," Kye explained, more worried than ever now for Derek.

The clerk scrunched his face in concentration and stared at the ceiling. Having apparently found the answer up there, he turned back to Kye. "You wanna take Allen Parkway to I-45 North and then merge to I-10 East heading toward Beaumont. It's not that far from here, really, but it's a different world."

Kye thanked the man and hurried out.

He spread the map beside him on the seat and found the streets Derek had mentioned. He arrived faster than he'd expected, in less than ten minutes. Yet in the short geographical distance he'd covered, it seemed as if he'd traveled to another country, leaving the Houston he knew behind. The trendy quirkiness of Montrose and the gracious elegance of River Oaks were replaced by rusty train tracks, crumbling warehouses and boarded-up, abandoned buildings.

He passed unpainted shotgun shacks collapsing in on themselves, scattered around a blocky brick building in front of which cars were still parked. It was, he assumed, the bar behind which Derek had been assaulted.

He spied Derek's car a little farther down the street and drove toward it, parking just behind it. Derek was in the driver seat, his head back, eyes closed, mouth open. For one horrible second Kye thought he was dead, but quickly realized he was only asleep.

He rapped sharply on the window and Derek opened his eyes and closed his mouth. He unlocked the door and opened it, tumbling out into Kye's waiting arms. His breath reeked of whiskey, his clothes of stale cigarette smoke and sweat. His shirt was ripped and several of the buttons were missing.

After making sure Derek's car was locked, Kye half-walked, half-carried him to Cassidy's car and helped him into the passenger seat. Even in his state of drunken dishevelment, Kye couldn't help but notice how good Derek looked.

"Should I take you to the ER? Get you checked out?"

"God, no." Derek was emphatic. "Just take me home. I think I'm more shook up than anything."

Kye drove carefully through the narrow streets in silence. He waited until they were on the freeway before probing further. "So, what happened, Derek? And what were you doing at a gay bar, anyway? I thought you'd turned one-hundred-percent het—engaged, set the date, the whole shebang."

Derek ran his hands over his face and rubbed his eyes. He looked at Kye and then out the passenger window. "I've missed you, Kye. You have no idea."

"I have some idea." Kye kept the hurt out of his voice, his eyes on the road.

"I really am happy with my life." Derek's tone became defensive. "It's the right thing for me. You'll never understand because you don't have the responsibilities and expectations placed on you that I have."

Kye didn't argue. It was a relief to admit he no longer felt the need to try to convince Derek of the error of his ways or to "save" him from himself. He just shook his head and continued to drive.

Derek went on. "But I need—uh—diversion from time to time. You know, just to blow off steam. No big deal. I love Brandy and all that, but sometimes, just for kicks, I want a little more. You know."

Kye didn't respond. Derek continued. "Tonight I thought I'd check out The Cesspool because it's in a part of town where I wouldn't risk running into anyone I know. Victor and Fred were really nice—at first. They're both body builders—super ripped. They kept buying me drinks. When they suggested we go out back, I figured we'd mess around a little. I didn't realize they had a lot more in mind than I was prepared for."

Derek's voice cracked and he put a fist to his mouth. He was breathing hard, clearly distressed. Kye felt sorry for him, but also angry at how stupid he was to go to some strange bar in a very bad neighborhood and let himself get picked up by two guys who could have killed him. He bit his tongue to keep from lecturing.

Derek spoke in an anguished voice, so quiet Kye had to strain to hear him. "They raped me. Both of them. They took turns. They did it dry. No condoms. They hurt me."

Compassion at once overrode all other emotions. "Jesus, Derek. I'm so sorry. So, so sorry that happened to you." He touched Derek's thigh. Derek grabbed his hand, squeezing so hard the college ring he wore cut into Kye's fingers. Derek was crying.

Kye let him cry, focused on getting them safely to Derek's townhouse. In a few minutes he pulled into the driveway and killed the engine. He extracted his hand from Derek's grip and got out of the car. He put his arm over Derek's shoulders as they walked toward the door.

"I keep a spare key hidden on the side of the house." The driveway was brilliantly lit by sensor floodlights. Kye waited while Derek found his key and returned. He noticed Derek was walking with a slight limp.

"I really think you should get yourself checked out. Especially because of the no condom thing. You owe it to your fiancée, if nothing else. You don't have to go to your regular doctor. Just go to some clinic. They don't care how prominent your family is." He knew he sounded bitter. He didn't care.

"I know." Derek dragged a weary hand over his face. "I know." He blew out a breath. "I'm going to. I promise."

"Good." Kye glanced at his watch. It was after three. "Listen, this isn't my car. I really need to get back—"

"No, no. Please don't go. Come inside, *please*. Just for a few minutes. I can't be alone. Not yet. Don't leave me." He turned those large puppy eyes on Kye, his expression pleading. Imagining the two bastards who took advantage of Derek's youth and innocence, ripping his clothing and taking turns holding him down while they raped him, made his heart surge with pain.

He entered the townhouse behind Derek, promising himself to stay only long enough to get him settled. They sat together on a large, comfortable sofa. Derek leaned in close, resting his head on Kye's shoulder.

As much to distract himself from the sweet, familiar weight of his ex-lover, Kye discussed practicalities. Derek had a second set of car keys. Once he was sober enough, he would need someone to go back out with him and get his car. Kye didn't volunteer for the job. Derek would need to get himself to a health clinic first thing as well, and make sure he followed up on the test results.

He began to lecture on safe sex and making wise choices when Derek twisted away and grabbed his head, pulling him down for a kiss. Stunned, Kye held himself still, but despite himself, he responded. All his carefully built defenses against Derek's charm were being breached as the kiss continued. He had forgotten the electric sparks Derek's kiss caused to dance over his skin, the softness of his long eyelashes brushing Kye's cheek, the burnished smoothness of his shaved cheek. His cock surged to attention.

He wrenched himself away. Nothing had changed. Everything had changed. This was not where he was supposed to be. Derek had made his choices and Kye had made a new life.

"No," he said firmly. "No." He was talking as much to himself as to Derek.

Derek tried to pull him down again. Kye pushed his hands away and stood. He stared down at Derek, angry at his audacity, angry at his own response. Gruffly he demanded, "What the fuck are you doing, Derek? What are you doing with your life? Don't marry this girl. You'll make her life and your own a living hell. You'll be living a lie."

Derek's face closed and he turned away. "You don't get it. You never did. I'm sorry. Thanks for the ride."

A thousand retorts tumbled through Kye's head, but none passed his lips. Derek was determined on his own path of self-destruction. If he didn't get killed in the process in his secret night-prowling. Derek was right. Kye didn't get it. He would never get choosing money and power, safety and comfort, over true happiness. Derek, he knew, would never be happy, yet that was the path he chose. The misery he would invariably encounter along the way would be of his own making.

As Kye drove back toward the house, one of his favorite quotes by the poet John Milton slipped into his mind. *The mind is its own place, and in itself, can make heaven of Hell, and a hell of Heaven.*

When he got home, Kye walked through the silent old house, tiptoeing up the stairs. He peeked in on Ian and Cassidy, who both appeared to be in a deep sleep. Instead of walking on down the hall back to his room, he stripped his clothing and lifted the sheets from the bottom of the bed, sliding up between the sleeping lovers, inserting himself in the middle of them.

Ian didn't move. He was lying on his back, an arm flung over his face. Cassidy turned toward him, half-opening one eye. "Kye." Her voice was thick with sleep. She draped herself over him, her warm, firm body enveloping him like a blanket, like a shield.

He stroked her thick, soft hair and closed his eyes. It felt good to be back with them, but would it ever feel like home?

Chapter Ten

"Hey, sleepyhead."

Kye opened one eye and squinted toward the sound of Cassidy's voice. She was leaning over him, her robe spilling open so he could see the curve of her bare breast. "What time is it?" he mumbled sleepily.

"After eleven. You never sleep this late. You okay?"

Kye opened the other eye and stretched his arms over his head, yawning. "Yeah. I'm fine. I got a call in the middle of the night from a friend in need. His car broke down. I left a note in case you woke up, but the two of you were still sleeping like logs when I got back."

"So that's what that note was. We were wondering, since you were sound asleep in bed, not out rescuing someone when we woke up." She peeled off the robe and slipped beneath the covers beside Kye. He stroked her breast, his cock rising as he watched her nipple stiffen and darken to his touch.

Leaning up, he bent over her and flicked the tender bud with his tongue. Cassidy sighed with pleasure, murmuring, "I love the way you do that."

"Hey, don't start without me." Ian stood in the doorway. He was shirtless, wearing his favorite denim cutoffs and nothing else.

"Are we starting something?" Kye leaned back. "Aren't you

supposed to be working? Isn't Brenda supposed to be here by now?"

"She's not coming today. She called in sick. But hey, I've been working really hard. Don't I deserve the reward of a morning off?" Ian unzipped his jeans and stepped out of them, revealing a rapidly rising cock beneath his briefs. "Unless"—he cocked an eyebrow and flashed an impish grin—"you object, boss." He slid beneath the sheets on Kye's other side.

"No objections here." Kye was actually glad for the distraction. He'd dreamt all morning of Derek, dreams filled with sun-drenched beaches and hours of idle lovemaking. He wanted to put that past him. Those dreams had nothing to do with reality.

Ian pulled back the sheets and wasted no time taking Kye's hard shaft between his lips. Cassidy watched them, her hand slipping between her legs, her eyes bright with lust. Kye groaned as Ian sucked him in deep. Though not yet as skilled as Cassidy, what he lacked in experience, Ian more than made up for in enthusiasm.

"Come here." Kye pulled Cassidy toward him, lifting her up over him. "Bring me that hot body. I want to taste you." Without a trace of her prior self-consciousness, Cassidy obediently positioned herself over his mouth, her knees on the bed on either side of his head.

Kye closed his eyes, inhaling her intoxicating feminine aroma. Teasingly he licked along her smooth outer labia, purposefully avoiding the inner petals and hooded pearl. Cassidy squirmed and sighed, settling her ass against his chest.

Ian continued to suck and stroke Kye's cock while Kye licked in slow, sensual circles toward Cassidy's clit. With feather-light strokes he teased her before finally pressing a finger into her soaked slit. Cassidy moaned and began to gyrate against his finger.

His kisses became more direct and intense, the way he knew she liked. He gripped her lush ass cheeks with both hands to hold her steady while he drove her into a frenzy of shudders and sexy gasps.

At the same time, Ian was driving Kye wild. He tried to hold on, waiting for Cassidy to come. All at once she began to tremble, chanting a sweet, breathy mantra. "Oh God, oh God, oh God..." He didn't stop lapping and suckling until she squealed and pushed hard at his shoulders.

He let her fall back and she rolled from his body, curling into a fetal position beside him, her cheeks, neck and chest mottled in orgasmic pink, her lips parted, her breasts heaving.

Ian, meanwhile, renewed his ardent attentions. It didn't take long before Kye shot his load, pleased at how expertly Ian swallowed every drop, not releasing his cock until he was completely spent. He lay limp, recovering for a few minutes, Cassidy curled against him, Ian kneeling back on his haunches beside him, his cock as straight and hard as a pointer's tail on the hunt.

Kye smiled at him and raised his eyebrows in question. "You've got choices here. How would you like your orgasm served this morning, Mr. Tanner?"

Ian grinned. "I want to feel Cass's hot pussy wrapped around my cock."

"That okay with you, Ms. Luke?"

Kye was secretly glad Ian wanted Cassidy and nothing more complex or inventive. His head was still foggy from sleeping so late. For the first time he wondered if the thrill was fading—a sure sign it would soon be time to move on. He pushed the thought aside as ridiculous. He was just tired, nothing more.

Cassidy uncurled her long, curvaceous body and held out her arms to Ian. Kye scooted down to the edge of the bed. "If you two don't mind, I'm going to hop in the shower." Neither minded, in fact they barely seemed to notice he had gone, intent on each other.

He peed in the shower and then soaped up, washing his hair and body, feeling more alive as the hot spray washed over him. His thoughts turned to Derek, which annoyed him. He'd done such a good job of wiping him from his mind that in the last month he'd gone days at a time without even thinking about him, and when he did, it was with a bittersweet sort of melancholy, not the ragged tear of pain he'd felt when he'd first left.

Now the wound he'd thought had healed was ripped open, and feelings he'd thought were gone had revived. What was his problem? He was too old for this shit. Infatuation and unrequited love were for teenagers, damn it. Not for a man soon to be twenty-nine.

He loved Cassidy and Ian, not some hypocritical kid barely into his twenties, engaged to a girl he was going to devastate because of his own inability to be honest with her, his family and most importantly, himself.

No, he loved the sexy couple making love in the other room, and knew they loved him as well. Not that that meant the three of them were glued at the hip—the proof right now demonstrated by the fact he could leave their bed to shower, without anyone feeling guilty or weird that the lovemaking continued without him.

Still, Derek had been through a rough time last night. Had he really been raped? Kye couldn't help but wonder, in retrospect. While he had definitely been drunk, he hadn't seemed especially traumatized for someone who had just been manhandled by two men in a dark alley. Yet his shirt had been ripped, the buttons missing, and when he'd first made that call, he had been scared, no question about it.

Maybe I'd better check in. Kye turned off the water and

stepped out of the shower. He dried himself, brushed his teeth and returned to the bedroom, tucking the towel around his waist. Cassidy and Ian were locked in an embrace, still in the throes of their lovemaking. Kye slipped silently past them and out the door.

Back in his bedroom, he flipped open his cell phone and called Derek. He got his voice mail. Just as well. What had he been thinking, anyway? Absently he pulled on a shirt and some jeans. Derek could take care of himself. Let him call Peggy Sue or whatever her name was.

Hungry, he walked back down the hall, planning to poke his head in and see if the lovebirds wanted a snack. He heard his name and stopped short.

He didn't mean to eavesdrop, yet found himself rooted to the spot, listening. Ian was speaking. "...not that I'm not crazy about Kye. He's terrific. But sometimes I just want you all to myself."

Cassidy was responding, but he couldn't make out her words. It was as if someone had dropped lead into his stomach. His periodic fears of being a third wheel burst into full flower. Ian was speaking again, though softer. Kye leaned forward, straining to hear. "...maybe get away a little. Just the two of us..."

"Kye? Is that you?"

He jerked back at the sound of Cassidy's voice, wondering if his shadow had given him away. Taking a breath, he moved forward and stepped inside the room. The couple was nestled in the bed together, cozy beneath the covers.

Kye no longer felt hungry. "I was just going out. I'll take my cycle. I won't be long." He had no idea where he was going—he just knew he had to get out.

"Don't forget your helmet," Cassidy clucked like a mother hen, as if he were a child, he thought irritably. He pushed the uncharitable thought aside. What was going on with him? Since when did he care if someone near him needed space? Hell, he was notorious in *his* need for space. Hadn't he traveled across two continents to find it?

Kye stepped outside into the muggy, sticky heat. He had purchased the small but peppy motorcycle a few weeks before from a friend of Ian's who was looking to buy something bigger. He'd applied for and obtained a Texas driver's license, something he'd been meaning to do for a while, though his international license was still in good standing.

He liked riding the cycle around town, zipping past long lines of cars at the red lights, though he was careful not to speed. He also liked having the freedom to get around without having to ask Cassidy for permission to drive her car. Not yet ready to make the commitment of owning an automobile himself, this motorcycle had seemed just the thing.

He rode aimlessly for a while, sticking to side roads with less traffic. He tried not to dwell on what he'd overheard. After all, it shouldn't come as any surprise. He'd burst into their lives and involved himself in every aspect. Perhaps he'd pushed himself where he wasn't wanted. Again the thought assailed him—maybe it was time to think about moving on. Nothing, he told himself philosophically, lasts forever.

He found himself in Derek's neighborhood, cruising along his street. Derek's car wasn't in the driveway, but it might still be sitting abandoned on McKee Street, if it hadn't been stolen in the meantime.

Kye pulled into the driveway, took off his helmet and hooked its strap over one handle. He strode to the door and rapped on it. There was no answer. He waited a minute and then rang the bell. He could hear some muffled sounds and thumping inside. He rang the bell again. "Derek. You in there? Open the door."

There was the scrape of the lock and the door handle

turned. "Brandy?"

Kye stiffened. "No. It's Kye. I wanted to make sure you were okay. You didn't answer your cell."

The door opcncd and there was Derek, his disheveled hair flopping over his eyes, squinting out into the sunlight. He was shirtless, still in the same pants he'd been wearing the night before. His face looked drawn and haggard, smudges of exhaustion beneath his eyes.

"Sorry. I was asleep. Man, what time is it?" He pushed his hair from his face and stepped back, opening the door wider to admit Kye.

"It's nearly two in the afternoon. You don't look so hot. Aren't you missing work?"

Derek shook his head. "Nah. I never bothered with that. I decided to take it easy before law school. It starts next week." He ran his hand over his face, pushing his hair from his forehead. "Man, I have some kind of hangover. Hoowee *dawg.*"

Kye snorted, amused at this Southern expression. He stepped into the townhouse, which felt chilly compared to the humid air outside. It was hard to believe he'd spent several weeks here, waiting like someone auditioning for a part for Derek to bring him fully into his life.

He shook away the memories. He was only here to see how Derek was doing after his harrowing night. Then he'd hit the road. "How are you today? You okay? Have you arranged for someone to go with you to get your car?"

"No. Maybe you could take me over?"

"I'm on a motorcycle. I don't have another helmet with me."

"Oh. Well. I'll take care of it later. You want a cup of coffee or something? My head feels like it's stuffed with cotton." He padded off toward the kitchen without waiting for Kye's response. Kye followed him.

He watched Derek pour water and spoon ground coffee beans into a coffeemaker. He seemed in pretty good spirits for someone who had been through what he'd been through. "You were in rough shape last night. Have you thought about pressing charges, Derek? Rape is a serious thing, whether it's done to a woman or a man."

Derek turned toward him, his expression incredulous. "*God*, no. Are you *kidding* me? I can just see the headline. *Son of prominent family files homosexual rape charges.*" He waved his hand through the air, as if the words appeared in a banner over his head. "Yeah, *right.*"

He removed the glass carafe from the coffeemaker, holding a mug beneath the flow of coffee until it was filled. He pushed the carafe back in place and leaned against the counter, sipping the brew, which Kye recalled he liked black.

Derek moved toward the table where Kye had sat down and slumped into a chair. "Anyway, I might have, uh, exaggerated what happened a little."

"What?" The penny dropped. He should have known.

"I mean, they didn't exactly, uh, rape me."

Kye pressed his lips together, waiting. Derek slurped noisily on his coffee and set it down, suddenly busying himself with a napkin.

Kye wasn't about to let him off that easy. "Go on."

"Well, uh. I mean, they *were* kind of rough. And I was drunk. But I went out to the alley with them willingly. I knew they wanted to fuck me." He was blushing hotly and refused to look up from his coffee mug.

"Did they use condoms?"

"No," came a whisper. "But it wasn't dry. One of the guys had lube."

"Why did you lie? Why call me in the middle of the night?

Why call *me* at all? Don't you have friends?"

"I—I really did lose my keys. And they had already taken off by the time I figured it out. I was too embarrassed to go back into the bar. I didn't know who to call. I mean, come on, look where I was, for God's sake. No one in my circle knows I'm—" Derek paused, searching for the word. *A flaming queer*, Kye wanted to shout, but he forced himself to stay quiet. "...sometimes into guys," Derek finished lamely.

He looked up finally at Kye. "I'm sorry I lied, Kye. I was pretty fucked up. Victor gave me some ecstasy. He said it would relax me." He sighed heavily and hung his head.

Kye didn't respond. He didn't move. He wasn't sure how he felt or what Derek expected of him. Derek looked up, his brilliant blue eyes bloodshot.

"I've missed you so much, Kye. I wanted to call a thousand times but I didn't figure it would do any good. I—I know I didn't treat you right. Things are different here in Texas. At least in my world. Anyway, I figured you'd probably be long gone, headed up to Austin to make your mark and all that." He squinted. "How come you're still here? What's kept you in Houston? Did you meet someone new?"

"Yeah, I did."

Kye didn't elaborate. Though he wasn't proud of himself for it, he rather liked the sudden spasm of pain that washed over Derek's face. God knows Derek had hurt him enough.

"A guy?"

"What's it matter, Derek? What's it matter to you, living in your rarified, homophobic, hypocritical little Texas elite world? What do you care what some Scottish faggot does on his own time, or who he does it with?"

Tears welled in Derek's eyes. "I'm sorry," he whispered, looking suddenly very young. He stood and Kye stood too, remorse following on the heels of his remark.

"Look." He tried to take away some of the pain still lingering on Derek's face. "I'm sorry. Things are what they are. Maybe someday they'll be different—for you, for me, I don't know. I'm glad you're okay and all that." He turned toward the door, desperate to be gone. "I have to go."

"No, wait. Please. Don't go."

"Why? What's left to say?"

"This." Derek pulled him close, pressing his hard body against Kye's. Derek's cock poked him and Kye's body responded in kind, despite the awkwardness of the situation.

Before he realized what was happening, Derek sank to his knees, fumbling at Kye's fly. He had Kye's cock out and into his mouth so quickly, Kye barely had a chance to protest.

He closed his eyes, just for a moment letting the hot, wet pleasure of Derek's eager mouth close over the crown. How ridiculous that he was still physically attracted to this idiot of a guy who pretty much lied to everyone he claimed to be close to, in order to get what he wanted.

Kye's mind short-circuited as Derek pushed his jeans and underwear down his thighs and cupped his balls with one hand, the other furiously pumping his shaft while he licked and kissed the head with lavish abandon.

Kye moaned. He knew he should push Derek away but it felt too damn good to stop him. Lazy days in Greece, where they'd spent hours making love, scrolled through his memory as Derek's hot mouth and urgent fingers played at his cock.

"We can still have this," Derek gasped as he came up briefly for air. "You and me. Secret rendezvous. You know you want me. You've never stopped wanting me."

Kye didn't answer. Instead he pushed Derek's head back down, forcing his cock deep into his throat. Derek gagged, but held on, again wrapping his hand around Kye's cock as he sucked him for all he was worth.

Just as he spurted his seed into Derek's willing mouth, a feminine screech startled them both. Derek fell back with a cry. Kye opened his eyes to see a petite woman with platinum blonde hair standing before them. She had a snub nose beneath wide blue eyes that were round with horror as she took in the sight before her.

"Oh God." Derek's voice was low and vibrant with panic. Kye pulled up his pants and tucked himself away, watching the drama unfold in front of him.

Derek scrambled to his feet. "Brandy! It's not what you think—"

"I *knew* it. You *bastard*. You fucking *faggot bastard*." Her voice, already high-pitched, rose to a squeal. "Morgan and Angela both told me they saw you at that gay bar on Elm Street and I told them they were crazy. All your bull about waiting till after marriage to have sex and I believed you. I thought it was romantic. You probably don't even *like* girls! I was just your front so you could fuck *men*."

She shot a look of such loathing toward Kye he almost started to protest his innocence as well. Instead he held up his hands in a helpless gesture. Despite her spewing rage, he couldn't help but feel sorry for the young woman. Her carefully constructed world was crashing down around her ears.

"Brandy, calm down. I can explain—" Derek's case wasn't helped by the dribble of Kye's semen at the corner of his mouth. Kye considered reaching out to wipe it away, but decided he didn't hate Derek that much.

Suddenly Brandy hurled herself at Derek, pummeling his chest with clenched fists, the large diamond on her left ring finger flashing, the red leather handbag over her arm swinging wildly. Kye briefly thought of intervening, but decided Derek could defend himself against the diminutive blonde. He'd worked hard to make this particular bed. Let him lie in it.

CஃB

Kye parked his motorcycle in the driveway and walked up the porch steps to the front door. Glancing at the floorboards, at one time painted dark red but now mostly bare wood, he thought again how they should sand and repaint the porch floor and railings. It would definitely give the old place a lift. He envisioned a cool, shiny gray. Once the weather cooled, they could get to work on it.

If you're still here.

Ignoring that voice for the time being, he opened the front door. He could hear voices raised. Cassidy and Ian were arguing about something. They were standing in Ian's studio, facing each other. Cassidy's hands were on her hips. Ian looked annoyed.

When they saw him, they both abruptly stopped the argument. Ian turned away. Cassidy's smile was over-bright. "Oh. Kye. We didn't hear you come in."

He knew with certainty they'd been arguing about him. Maybe a continuation of the earlier overheard discussion? Ian wanted him out. Why didn't he have the balls to say it to his face?

He knew that wasn't fair. Kye would accomplish nothing by forcing issues they weren't yet ready to discuss. Hadn't he himself been having second and third thoughts? Had he said a word to them about it?

Still, the probability that they were discussing it, discussing *him*, made him distinctly uncomfortable. He continued to walk past the pair, waving his hand casually. "Don't let me interrupt. I'm just going to get some sauce started for the ravioli."

Cooking calmed his nerves, and soon, lost in the chopping of onions, garlic and fresh tomatoes, the tension that had bunched in his shoulders eased a bit. He opened a bottle of wine and poured himself a glass.

Cassidy entered the kitchen a few minutes later. "It smells good in here."

"It's the garlic and onions." He pointed toward the pan on the stove, where the vegetables were sautéing in virgin olive oil. He poured Cassidy a glass of wine. He wanted to ask her what she and Ian had been arguing about, but he didn't. Instead he opened cans of tomato paste and sauce, dumping them into a large pot. He poured in some of the red wine from the bottle and added fresh chopped oregano, along with other spices.

"So, whose car broke down last night? You should have woken us up. Ian would have gone with you."

Kye smiled. "You were both sleeping like the dead. There was no reason to disturb you. I took care of it."

"Was it Derek?"

Kye turned back toward the stove, aware his face was heating. "Aye."

Cassidy's voice was small. "And today? You went to see him?"

"Look, Cassidy." He whirled toward her. "What I do in my spare time..." She looked so timid, biting her lip, her eyes wide. He was at once contrite. "I'm sorry. I—I guess I'm a little sensitive about him still. Yes—I went to see him. To make sure he was all right. He, uh, he got pretty drunk last night and lost his car keys. I was just making sure he got through the night okay."

Cassidy nodded and sipped her wine. He knew she wanted to ask more—to ask if he planned to see Derek again and how it would affect things between them. He wanted to talk about it. And about Ian's overheard remark, and whatever they'd been arguing about when he walked in, but he didn't. Somehow he couldn't bring himself to say a word. Maybe he was afraid of the answers he would hear, afraid of what he might say in response.

∞

Something was wrong, but Ian couldn't put his finger on what. Kye was unusually quiet at dinner. Most evenings he regaled them with tales of his travels and adventures. Ian loved to listen to his stories. He would have loved to listen to Kye read the phonebook—Ian couldn't get enough of his rich, rolling brogue.

Cassidy had mentioned earlier that Kye had admitted to going to see his old lover, Derek someone or other. Cassidy didn't like it that he'd gone to see him. She said he acted strange afterward, but she hadn't had the nerve to probe too much, as he clearly hadn't wanted to talk about it.

Ian had mixed feelings about it. On the one hand, he secretly liked the idea that Kye didn't consider himself so much a part of their relationship that he couldn't step out now and again with someone else. It gave Ian the advantage with Cassidy, or so it seemed to him. He was the rock, the one she could rely on, no matter what.

On the other hand, he'd felt a strange stab of jealousy when she'd told him. The image of Kye in the arms of another man gave him an odd, uncomfortable feeling. Kye belonged with them. Weren't they enough for him? He knew these feelings were contrary and irrational, and tried not to dwell on them. Kye was a free man. He could do what he liked.

After dinner, Cassidy went out with her sister and a girlfriend she hadn't seen in a while. They were going to some chick flick and then out for a drink. "Don't wait up, boys." She winked.

Ian did the dishes while Kye finished some work on the laptop in the kitchen nook. The old house hadn't come equipped with a dishwasher, but Ian didn't mind. He found the washing and drying of dishes to be kind of soothing.

He glanced toward Kye, who seemed intent on whatever he was doing. A sudden fantasy flashed through his mind. Wouldn't it be fun to slip beneath the desk and distract the hell out of him while he tried to work? Did he dare? Ian was rarely the instigator when it came to sex with Kye. While confident with a woman, he was still somewhat shy when it came to men.

He poured and drank some more wine and watched Kye working for a while. Knowing Cassidy wouldn't come bursting in on them gave him more courage. While he enjoyed sucking cock, he knew he was nowhere near as skilled at it as she was, and didn't want to be compared.

His own cock rose hard against his belly as his plan formed in his head. He wiped his hands on a dishtowel and moved toward Kye. "Excuse me." He tried not to grin. "I dropped something under the desk. No, you don't have to get up. Just let me get down here a minute."

He maneuvered himself into the space under the desk, between Kye's legs. Kye pushed his chair back. "Hey, what're you doing down there?"

Without answering, Ian leaned forward, placing his hands on Kye's strong, bare thighs. He drew his tongue along Kye's inner thigh until his nose touched Kye's denim-covered crotch.

"I found what I was looking for." Ian looked up with a sly grin. His heart was beating fast. "It's just in here. If I can only get to it." He jerked at the metal buttons that held Kye's fly closed. To his surprised dismay, Kye slid his chair back farther and put his hand on Ian's head, pushing him away.

"Sorry. I've really got to finish this report. The quarterly taxes are due in a few days and I have to calculate how much we owe. Can I take a rain check?"

Ian flushed. He was mortified to have been rebuffed. Sitting up abruptly, he bumped his head hard against the bottom of the desk.

"Ouch," Kye offered in sympathy. "You okay? You want some ice?"

"I'm fine," Ian snapped, humiliated. "Sorry to interrupt your work." He escaped from the kitchen as quickly as he could, waiting until he was in his studio before rubbing the bump that was rising on his head. He wished Cassidy was there to comfort him. No—he was glad she hadn't been there to witness his humiliation.

He sat at his worktable and tinkered for a few minutes with some new pieces he was working on, but found he couldn't concentrate. Instead he went upstairs and changed from shorts to a pair of jeans. He put on a fresh shirt and splashed some cologne on his neck. When he came back downstairs and stuck his head in the kitchen, Kye was still at his computer.

"I'm going down to Jim's Place." Ian turned away so he wouldn't have to see Kye's face. "Catch ya later." Before Kye could reply, he was gone.

Chapter Eleven

Cassidy sat still, trying to process what Kye had just said. Surely she'd misheard him. Leaving? For how long? Why? What had they done? How could he just go? How would they get along without him? Who would handle the business end of things? Who would make love to them both until they melted with pleasure?

"You're leaving?" she finally managed to say, her voice sounding strangely distant in her own ears. Hot tears threatened to spill. She blinked them back.

She turned to Ian, who looked as if he'd been sucker-punched, his face registering the same shock she felt.

"It's not forever. You know I've been meaning to check out the music scene in Austin. And, I don't know." He paused and blew out a big breath. "I just need...some time. To figure things out."

Things had been going so well—the three of them were great together in every way—as friends, lovers, business partners. What had gone wrong? Was he leaving them for another couple? The idea was so ludicrous she would have grinned, except it wasn't funny.

Now she recalled his midnight visit to his ex-lover, and how oddly he'd behaved upon his return. Yes, ever since early in the week he'd been different—sort of reserved, even distant. Was he leaving them for him? Unable to hold her tongue, Cassidy demanded, "Is it your ex-lover? Derek? Is that who you're going back to, now that you're tired of us?"

Kye reddened and Cassidy knew she'd hit a nerve. He'd never really talked about the guy he'd left the very day he'd come home with her. He'd talked in vague terms about meeting him in Greece and following him back to Texas, but as far as she'd known, it had been a clean break between them.

God only knew what had *really* happened the other night when he'd rescued him in his stranded car. For all she knew, the love affair had been rekindled. The possibility made her stomach hurt so much she clutched at it, grimacing.

The three of them were sitting at the kitchen table having breakfast. It was Friday, and usually they didn't sit down for a formal breakfast except on Sundays, but Kye had told the two of them he needed to discuss something. As usual, he'd made something delicious—this time fresh biscuits and grilled ham, served with butter and maple syrup.

Kye put a hand on Cassidy's arm. "Please, Cassidy. Try to understand. I'm not leaving you for someone else." His voice was gentle. "I'm not leaving you at all. I'm not abandoning the business. I'll take my laptop with me to handle the business end of things from Austin. I'll have my cell, too. It's just..." He paused, looking down. "I need some time to figure some things out." He glanced up at Ian and back toward her. "And you two— maybe you need some space as well. As a couple."

"Why would we need space?" Cassidy knew she sounded petulant but she couldn't help it. "We love having you here. Don't we, Ian?" She turned to him for confirmation. He nodded but then looked away.

"Please, Cassidy," Kye implored. "Don't make this harder than it has to be."

"How long?" Ian's voice was quiet, subdued. He was staring into his cup, which he held with both hands. Cassidy could see he was upset too, but was keeping it in, in typical Ian fashion.

"A week. Maybe two. I don't know. I'll keep in touch." Kye put his hands behind his head and looked up at the ceiling. Cassidy could see this wasn't easy for him, but that didn't make her feel any better. Yes, something had definitely been off all week, though she hadn't been too worried until now, figuring things would sort themselves out.

"What will you do in Austin?" Ian's voice was neutral.

"Check out the music scene, like I was going to do before I met you. Play a few open mics, see how I like the place. I don't know. Something always comes up."

Cassidy stared from one man to the other. They were acting like this was all perfectly fine. Kye could just drop into their lives, change everything and then waltz away, off to his next adventure, his next conquest. How could he leave them? How come Ian seemed so unfazed by it all? Was she the only one who cared? Had it been nothing more than casual sex for the guys?

She opened her mouth and closed it again. Maybe things were as Kye claimed. Maybe he needed a little time and space apart, for whatever damn reason. In a week or two he'd come home again and everything would be fine and dandy.

And then again, maybe he wouldn't.

The tears she'd managed to hold back until now spilled over. Pushing back her chair, she ran from the room.

03

"You asleep?" Cassidy's voice penetrated Ian's brooding reverie. He looked at the clock beside the bed. It was nearly three in the morning.

"No."

"You think he'll come back?"

"Time will tell, I guess."

Kye had been gone for four days. As promised, he had kept in touch by email and cell phone. Whatever he did with cash flow, bills and accounts receivable, he was apparently able to do just as well from afar, at least for the time being.

He had called them each evening, giving them updates about his activities, discussing aspects of the business that needed his attention and checking in on how they were doing. The conversations were breezy, impersonal and short. Ian understood this was just Kye's way, indeed the way of most men, who didn't like to chat on the phone any longer than they could help it.

It bothered Cassidy more. "How can he just act like everything's fine?" She frowned. "He sounds so—happy. I mean, it isn't fair. Did we really mean so little to him?"

"I don't think it's that," Ian had tried to tell her, though he himself was also hurt by Kye's sudden departure. "I think he really does need some time. You know, if you think about it, we shouldn't be surprised. It's not like he ever pretended to be something he's not. He told us when we met him he was a gypsy. He's twenty-eight and never settled down, not even in one place, much less with one person."

"Or two," Cassidy interrupted with a grin, and Ian was glad to see she could still find humor in things.

"Yeah." He grinned back. "Or two."

Though Ian hadn't admitted it to Cassidy, at first he'd been almost glad when Kye announced he was going to take off for a while. He'd been avoiding Kye in the few days leading up to Kye's announcement, still embarrassed and humiliated by his rejection.

It seemed so unfair. Cassidy wouldn't have bungled it like he had. She would have instinctively known the right moment for her seduction. Kye would have too. It had been especially painful, because up to the moment when Kye blew him off, he'd felt so adventurous, so sexy and reckless. Kye's rebuff reminded him why he rarely made the first move in any relationship. It would be a while before he tried anything like that again.

When he had more time to think about it, Ian recognized Kye's reaction probably wasn't a direct rebuff. He was clearly preoccupied, probably already thinking about making a break.

What had really precipitated his leaving? Had he reunited with his ex-lover as Cassidy had first suspected, or moved on to find someone new? Ian didn't think so. He thought back carefully over the events leading up to Kye's leaving. He'd seemed most upset that Monday, taking off for several hours on his own, without saying where he was going. That wasn't like Kye.

The timing was ironic, since Ian had just been saying that morning to Cassidy he thought maybe they should get away themselves, just the two of them...

Holy shit.

Kye had been outside the bedroom door—they had seen his shadow. Had he overheard that conversation? Was that why he left? He didn't think he was wanted? He glanced at Cassidy. Did he tell her? Would she then blame him for Kye's leaving? Would she be right to?

Maybe it was even more basic. Maybe Kye was just ready to move on, and there was nothing Cassidy or he could have done about it. True, things were complicated by Kye's share in the business, but Ian knew Kye could be fairly easily replaced by anyone with a degree in business and a good head on their shoulders.

But Kye himself could never be replaced. Not only the scorching hot sex, but the great music and the lively conversations. Not to mention his cheerful smile and his cool

Scottish accent. Ironically, Ian found himself wishing he could talk to Kye about all this. He missed how well Kye could listen—his whole self completely focused on the topic at hand. He was so easy to talk to and never judged or criticized. Ian felt safe telling him things he might not even share with Cassidy.

Even in a situation that could have potentially sparked terrible jealousies, it was Kye who kept things moving on an even, comfortable keel. Looking back, Kye had never given him reason to feel jealous or insecure when the three of them were together. Kye never seemed to favor Cassidy over himself. He was generous with his love and affection and seemed equally happy in the arms of either lover. Cassidy, too, while definitely into Kye, made her loving feelings for Ian clear at every turn.

And yet...and yet Ian had to admit, on a certain level, one he didn't tap into or acknowledge very often, he had sometimes been threatened by Kye's presence in their relationship. Now he wondered why.

Because you wanted him too much.

Whoa.

Ian sat up abruptly. Where did that come from? But it was true. Jesus, it was true. He had been so hurt when Kye turned him away. Though he'd tried to tell himself it didn't matter, it had cut him to the quick.

"What is it? You okay?" Cassidy stirred beside him.

"I think I just figured something out."

"What?" She turned toward him expectantly. For a moment he regretted saying anything. Over the years, especially when they were operating under his enforced rules of "just friends", his first impulse when uncomfortable with something was to say nothing—to deny it, both to himself and to Cassidy. He wanted to protect her, or probably closer to the truth, himself. Instead of giving of himself completely, he held back, afraid of being judged and found wanting.

Well, he didn't want to be that man anymore. He *wasn't* that man anymore. He took a deep breath and blew it out. He had two things to tell her. He would begin with the easier one, the one less close to the bone of his emotions. "Remember last Monday when I was saying maybe you and I should have more time alone? Maybe get away for a time, just the two of us?"

"Yeah." She sat up and stared at him. Her eyes widened and she put a hand to her mouth. "Oh my God! Do you think he overheard that? Shit! I bet he did. He was right there, in the hallway. Do you think he left because you said that? Do you think he got the impression we don't want him around because of that?"

"Man, I hope not. I would feel awful if that was the reason. But I've thought about it a lot, Cass. I don't think that's it. Or at least it's certainly not the only thing. He's a wanderer. He told us that from the start. He doesn't stay in one place for very long. It was probably just a matter of time before he moved on. That remark, if overheard, probably just hurried things up a bit."

Cassidy began to cry, tears rolling down her cheeks. Ian pulled her down to his chest and stroked her hair. "Shh, don't cry, baby. I know you miss him horribly. I do too." As much to distract her as anything, he hurried on. "I have something more important to tell you. Something about me. About us. I want to share it. I want you to help me understand it."

As he had hoped, Cassidy quieted. Her face was wet against his chest. He pulled her up beside him and, using a corner of the sheet, wiped her cheeks. "Listen. You know how much I love you, right?" Cassidy nodded. "And I know you love me too." Again she nodded. "So you know me probably better than anyone. You know I tend to shut down my real feelings sometimes because it's easier just to go with the flow, stay superficial and thus safe. It's what I did to you, for which I'm so sorry. I wanted us to stay just friends because I was afraid if we

147

were more, then I would fuck it up and it would be over and I would lose you forever.

"But I'm different now. Or I hope I am. I don't want to run and hide from feelings just because they're scary. I want to embrace life fully, and love as well. If Kye comes back or if he doesn't, I don't want to be the kind of person I used to be."

Cassidy put her hand to his cheek, her touch soft and encouraging. "That's wonderful, Ian. You should know, too, that I'm very happy with our new relationship. If Kye isn't going to be a part of it anymore, we'll just have to muddle through on our own." She laughed and wiped another tear that spilled sweetly over her cheek. Ian's heart ached with love and compassion.

He closed his eyes, trying to articulate his thoughts. "That said, I want to fess up." He tried to grin and didn't quite manage it. "Even though it was really sexy and fun with Kye, sometimes I felt jealous. I was afraid you would prefer him over me. I mean, who could blame you?"

Cassidy started to protest but he held up a hand. "No, I wasn't fishing for a compliment there, I swear, and you don't need to answer. What I'm trying to say is, I didn't always tell you when I was nervous or uncomfortable—I pretty much just put my head down and pushed my way through it. You know, like a man." Now he did manage a grin and Cassidy smiled back.

"But it goes deeper than that. I wasn't just afraid of losing you, or being shown up by Kye as a lover. Lying here just now, I realized the reason why I was sometimes uncomfortable with the intensity of our ménage. It's not because Kye is too into you, or you're too into him." He paused and then hurried on before he lost the will to continue. "It's me. I'm afraid *I've* been too into Kye."

"What?" Cassidy tilted her head, her expression quizzical. "I'm not sure I get what you're saying."

"I've never had that kind of emotional connection with a guy, you see. I mean, there were guys from time to time, as you know, but it was really more about the sex. I liked the guys and all, but I certainly didn't...love them." There, he'd said it aloud. Determined to keep going, to honestly and openly express himself to the woman he claimed to love above all else, Ian continued.

"What I'm trying to say is I love Kye. I'm in love with Kye." Wow, it felt really strange to say that out loud. Yet it also felt good—freeing. He was being completely honest for once—baring himself to the bone. "I never said it before—not to him, not to you, not to myself. Because it freaks me out, I guess. I mean, does this make me gay? If I can love a man, does this mean I'll stop loving you? Can a person even be in love with two people at the same time? Can something like this possibly sustain itself? Or was it just a matter of time before one of us bailed?"

Leaning up on her elbow, Cassidy smiled her angel's smile at him, making him smile back, despite his lingering confusion. "You know what Kye would say about your fears of being gay, right?"

"No, what would he say?"

"He'd say, why label yourself? He'd say follow your heart and your desires and just be yourself. If others feel like they have to call you something or define you in some way, that's their problem. Look at the three of *us*." She gave a small, snorting laugh. "When I told Jane about it—that we were becoming serious, she freaked out. I mean, she was cool with sex between three, but *love*? She told me from the start it couldn't last, but I think she's wrong. Even now, with him gone, I think she's wrong. Gay, bi, straight, whatever the three of us are, we *work* together."

She squeezed his arm. "I *love* watching you and Kye together. It's *so* hot. But I honestly never thought of either one of you as gay, or even bi for that matter. What I mean is, I just

149

don't think about it. It doesn't matter.

"And as to your other question, of *course* you can be in love with two people at the same time. What the hell do you think has been going on over the last months? We've all three been falling in love with each other. I know he loves us both, I just *know* it." The smile fell away from her face and the tears welled again. "That's why it hurts so much to have him gone."

ɕʒ

Kye was alone on the stage, perched on a stool, his guitar in his arms, leaning toward the microphone. The room was crowded and several people near the bar at the back of the room were talking loudly, obviously drunk. That was one reason why he generally preferred to play coffeehouses rather than bars, because there the people came expressly for the music, instead of using it as background to their drunken conversations.

Still, there were several filled tables near the stage, and the people sitting at them were quiet, their expressions rapt as they listened to the music. He was singing one of his favorite songs, "Bee's Wing" by Richard Thompson, the irony of the lyrics not lost on himself. Like the girl in the song, he was a gypsy, running from love.

When he came to the break, more of the room quieted. That was always his goal by the end of a set—to see how many people he could get into the music.

He finished the song and after a moment's pause, the room burst into hearty, enthusiastic applause. He smiled and stood, the three-song limit having been met. The M.C. ran up to the stage and thumped him on the back. His accent was so thickly Texan that Ian had a hard time understanding him.

"Hope y'all wull come on back, ya hear? That was Kyle McMillian, y'all. Give him 'nuther show of our 'presheashun.'"

Kye was only mildly annoyed the man had gotten his name wrong. It wasn't like this was a paid gig—just an open mic for anyone with a guitar and the nerve to get up and make music.

As he stepped off the stage, a young woman came toward him. She had long, very straight blonde hair and wore a tie-dye tank top and a flowing cotton skirt streaked with color. Her breasts, he couldn't help noticing, were not confined by a bra. Though the breasts themselves were small, the nipples were prominent against the sheer fabric of her top, and he tried not to stare, focusing instead on her face.

"You were terrific." Her voice was breathless with admiration and she enthusiastically squeezed his arm. "Just great. Your guitar work during the break on that last song was phenomenal. Did you write that?"

He smiled. "Don't I wish. But thank you. You're very kind." He eyed the bar, eager for a pint of something. Performing always left him a little giddy, and a beer or strong ale helped to calm his nerves.

"Oh my God," she squealed. "I *love* your accent. Why is it Brits never sing with an accent?"

"I'm Scottish, actually."

"Oh, well. Whatever." She tossed her head dismissively, as if the distinction was barely worth mentioning. Kye was amused but said nothing. "Anyway, I hope you're sticking around, because my band is going up soon, and we are *desperate* for a lead guitar."

Kye continued to push through the crowd toward the bar. The girl trailed behind him. "My name's Summer." He turned back toward her, arching an eyebrow. She was, he guessed, maybe eighteen, twenty at the most. "Well," she admitted, "my given name is Linda, but that's so yesterday. Our band's called

Pop Rocks. You know, after that weird candy that, like, explodes in your mouth?"

Kye didn't know but he nodded, aware he wouldn't get a word in edgewise even if he wanted to. He gestured toward the barman and placed his order. He considered offering to buy Summer a drink, but nixed the idea. She was probably underage.

"So anyway," she went on. "We have a lead singer, that would be me." She flashed a dimpled smile. She really was quite attractive, though she didn't hold a candle to Cassidy, he thought with a sudden pang. "And we have a drummer, Zach, he's insane. But all drummers are insane. You probably know that. Then we have Gordon—he plays bass and he's really good on keyboard too. He writes most of our stuff. I do some too, just the lyrics, and he puts the music to it. We used to be together, you know, but we broke up. We have a rhythm guitar guy, Mike, but he can't do lead. He's great for keeping the beat, not to mention he owns all the sound equipment, but we really need someone who can take off, you know? Who can turn us from a good to a great band. Do you write your own stuff?"

He waited a beat, in case she wasn't finished with her stream of consciousness. She had closed her mouth, however, and was looking at him expectantly, so he answered. "Sometimes. Not much lyrics though. I have a lot of instrumental stuff. But I'm not really looking—"

"No, don't say it!" She put her hands over her ears and squeezed her eyes shut. He closed his mouth and waited. She opened her eyes and fixed him with a pleading gaze. "Don't say anything. Not yet. Just hear us first. Then you can tell me all your reasons why you aren't looking to join a band, and even if you were, ours would be dead last on the list." She laughed and he smiled back in spite of himself. She had guts, if nothing else.

"Can I get you a drink? A soda or something?"

She pursed her lips in a pleasing pout. "You think I'm too

young to drink, don't you? It's okay, I'm used to it. Actually I'm twenty-four, but I've never looked my age. But no thanks on the drink. I never drink alcohol before a gig. I'd forget the words. But afterwards I've been known to toss back one or three." She giggled.

The woman who had been introduced to the stage after Kye, finished her set to scattered applause. Kye realized guiltily he hadn't paid a bit of attention. Summer had captured it all. A man and a woman went up next. The man played an out-of-tune banjo while the woman sang a few country tunes in a nasally twang that did nothing for Kye.

"We're up next," Summer whispered urgently, gripping his arm again in an earnest clutch. "It's Kyle, right?"

"Actually it's Kye. Kye McClellan."

"Kye." She caressed the word. "Cool. Weird but cool." She continued to clutch his arm. "Don't go, okay? I'll check back after, okay? Promise?"

"Aye. I'll be right here." He held up his ale and smiled.

She let him go and stepped back, appraising him with tilted head. "God, I just *love* the way you talk. Not to mention the way you *look.*"

He smiled but said nothing. She might claim to be twenty-four but he had his doubts.

"I've gotta go round up my boys. See you in twenty." She disappeared into the crowd, shiny blonde hair and flowing skirts flying.

愉

Trying not to disturb her, Kye disentangled himself from the naked girl entwined around him. He'd known it was a mistake to go home with her, but several beers and a very persistent girl had blunted his judgment.

Her band turned out to be surprisingly good. Summer's singing voice was smoky and dark and the songs they performed were original and interesting, though they tended to go on too long. Like most beginning musicians, they lacked the discipline to cut and arrange, too in love with their own stuff to be critical.

After the open mic, he agreed to go with them to Mike's house. Mike had a pretty decent sound system, set up in the living room of a house he rented with Gordon and two other guys near the University of Texas campus.

Kye jammed with them for an hour or so. It was fun and they enthusiastically urged him to join the band, but he wasn't ready to commit. If he were honest, he wasn't even sure what the hell he was doing in Austin.

He'd known when he gave Summer a ride back to her place on his motorcycle that she'd invite him in. He'd known she would expect him to seduce her. He hadn't, pleading exhaustion, which wasn't altogether untrue.

He'd slept his first three nights in Austin in a cheap motel on a lumpy mattress, tossing and turning, awakening to reach for Ian or Cassidy, for a split second confused to find they weren't there.

She'd accepted his polite refusal to fuck her with a laugh and toss of her head, and opened the futon couch in her small living room for him to sleep on. He hadn't been surprised when she'd crept, naked, into his sheets about an hour later. He was awake, but pretended to be asleep. But when she scooted down in search of his cock, he pulled her up into his arms.

"Not tonight, lass. I'm sorry."

"Is it another girl?"

"Aye. You could say that."

Summer sighed loudly. "Figures. The good ones are either

taken or gay. Where is she? How come you're not with her?"

"Taking a bit of a break." He was not about to tell her his story. "Breathing space, I guess you could say."

"For her or you?"

"To tell you the truth, I don't know anymore."

She seemed to accept this, for which he was glad. He wasn't in the mood to talk, especially not about Cassidy and Ian.

"Hold me, then," she commanded with the bossiness perfected by pretty young girls accustomed to getting what they want. "I'm lonely."

Me too. Summer curled her warm, soft body into his side. He wrapped his arms around her and kissed the top of her head. Her hair smelled like baby shampoo. Soon her breathing became deep and regular.

Slipping from the bed, he went out onto the porch to stare up at the night sky filled with stars, far more stars than he could see in the Houston sky. He settled himself on the lone chair, a rocker that had once been painted white, most of it now worn down to the wood. He rocked back and forth, wrapping his arms around himself for comfort. The knowledge that there was a naked girl lying asleep just inside, a girl he could have for the plucking if he wanted her, only made him lonelier still.

He missed Ian and Cassidy a ridiculous amount. Yet he couldn't get the words he'd overheard between them out of his head. *...sometimes I just want you all to myself...maybe get away a little. Just the two of us...*

When he'd told them he was leaving, he could have sworn Ian looked relieved, if not exactly happy. It wasn't only that one overheard conversation that had tipped his decision. He wasn't blind. Cassidy and Ian were a couple. Maybe it had taken his coaxing to make them realize it, but in the end, he was just someone passing through. How could he be more?

Beyond all that, he knew it wasn't fair to blame the whole thing on that one overheard conversation, or even on the shared history of the pair. He knew, at his core, it was the way he was hardwired. That's how it had always been in his life—he was destined to be the one passing through. He was a gypsy, a wanderer, always seeking something new. But there was a price to pay for always being the one to leave—and the price this time, maybe for the first time, suddenly seemed too high.

He glanced at the dark sky. It was late, far too late to call Ian and Cassidy. They'd probably been asleep for hours anyway. With a sigh, he hoisted himself from the rocker and slipped silently back into the darkened room. To his relief, Summer had disappeared from his bed. He lay down, certain he wouldn't sleep, but eventually he did.

Cප

"We haven't had a break from the business in months. A couple of days won't hurt anything. I don't know about you, but I could use a change of scenery. Come on, let's do it."

Cassidy was surprised Ian wanted to take a vacation, even if it was only for a few days. Since he'd thrown himself into their jewelry business, he often worked seven days a week, sometimes for twelve or fourteen hours a day. True, things had eased up for him since they had hired Brenda. He was teaching her some of the more complex techniques now, and Brenda showed a flare for design. Ian had joked soon the business wouldn't need him.

"So where did you have in mind?" She came up behind his chair and peered over his shoulder. He pointed to the computer screen. *Fair Acres Bed & Breakfast—Tucked away in the Hill Country on the shores of beautiful Lake Travis, this 1863 English country house was part of an original homestead of the Republic of Texas. Ideal for romantic getaways, yet close enough to enjoy Austin's urban, eclectic nightlife.*

The photographs of the house and the lake were tantalizing, and the rooms looked elegant yet cozy. The price was a little steep, but Ian persisted.

"Come on. We've earned it. Kye says we're turning a steady profit now. Let's live a little. It'll be romantic."

"And you happened to pick something near Austin because...?" She raised her eyebrows.

Ian flushed but didn't deny it, for which she was glad. He missed Kye as much as she did. Though he talked about it less, nothing was the same without Kye around.

There was the obvious stuff they missed. No more home-cooked meals, though Cassidy tried her hand at a few recipes he'd shown her. Nothing came out nearly as well as when he made it. And, as odd as it seemed, the kitchen table was too big now. When they sat together for dinner, they both felt his absence more keenly than during the rest of the day, when they could almost pretend he was just running an errand, or in the other room, or maybe out on the porch strumming his guitar.

That morning when the bank had called with a question about their financial statements, Cassidy had had to tell them she would get back to them, instead of handing Kye the phone. She knew she had come to rely on him too much and too quickly regarding the financial side of the business, but she'd always hated all that accounting stuff. It had been such a relief to be able to trust someone who not only understood it, but enjoyed it.

For the hundredth time since he'd gone, she wondered how he could have just up and left them. Why, she also wondered, had he let himself get in so deep first? Not only with them as lovers, but with Ian Tanner Designs? He owned a third of the company. They'd made it official, signing new documents adding him as a partner and filing the papers with the State of Texas. Did he plan to run things by phone and email forever? Or was he going to bail on the business too, just when things were taking off?

In her heart of hearts, though, Cassidy didn't care about that so much. What she missed most of all were the nights. The incredible, hot sex, yes of course that. But even more, she missed falling asleep between her two men, feeling so safe and secure, so loved.

She was still happy with just Ian—she wouldn't deny that. If it hadn't been for Kye, she would still be sleeping down the hall, frustrated and miserable. But Kye had made things that much better, that much more thrilling and alive. For the first time in her life she had felt complete, with no desire for anything but what she had.

Ian answered her teasing question with surprising directness. "Yes," he admitted quietly. "I want to be near Kye. Maybe we could see him. You know, just casually mention that we're in the area when he calls. Get together for a beer maybe, see how he's doing. Something very low key. What do you think?"

The thought of seeing him again—those silver gray eyes that could capture and hold her like no one else, the rakish, dimpled grin that made her grin back, no matter what mood she was in—caused an actual pain in her heart. She put her hand to her chest in a vain effort to ease it.

"I think"—she leaned over Ian and wrapped her arms around him—"it's a *great* idea." She refused to consider the possibility he might refuse to see them. She would think positive thoughts, hope for the best, and leap in with both feet. "Can we go tonight?"

Chapter Twelve

"It's Kye. Should I get it?" Cassidy held up the ringing cell phone. It was a little after noon on a Wednesday. They hadn't seen Kye for five days. They were heading northwest on Route 71, having managed to procure reservations for the bed & breakfast. Cassidy was excited and infused with a sense of purpose. After drifting around for the past several days feeling lost and confused, at least they were doing *something*.

"Yeah, get it, but don't tell him where we are. Not yet." Ian kept his eyes on the road but Cassidy saw he was smiling. She hadn't seen him smile much since Kye had disappeared.

"Hello?"

"Cassidy. It's Kye."

"Hi there. How's it going?"

He seemed to hesitate before saying, "Okay, I guess." Cassidy felt a sudden flare of hope that he might be unhappy, and ready to come home, but he made no such declaration. His tone was matter-of-fact, his words all business. "I wanted to let you know I'm making a transfer of funds to pay for the raw materials you ordered last week. There's money in the account to cover it so we won't have to draw up the line."

"Okay." Cassidy grinned at Ian. She was like a kid with a big secret. She was dying to blurt it out. *We're coming to see you! Tell us where you are.* Instead she answered his few questions about the website and other mundane business issues. Cassidy kept her tone casual. "So, what's on your plate today? Any plans for tonight?"

"Yeah, actually. I kind of hooked up with this band. Just a short-term thing. They have a gig at Bradley's tonight down in the warehouse district. Rumor has it a couple of music industry bigwigs will be there scoping out the talent. They're just kids, but they have a lot of potential. I agreed to sit in for a night or two."

"Bradley's down in the warehouse district," Cassidy repeated, casting a meaningful look at Ian that said, *pay attention.* "That sounds great. Didn't take long to find a band to perform with, huh? Not that I'm surprised, with your phenomenal talent."

Kye laughed. "Thanks for your vote of confidence, love. It's been a while, though. I'm still getting used to playing with a group. It's a different mindset than being on your own. Not to mention I'm trying to learn their entire set list in the space of a few hours." He laughed again, the sound warm.

"I miss you both," he offered, at the precise moment Cassidy said, "We miss you so much."

Cassidy sighed. She hadn't meant to say that. No pressure—she and Ian agreed if they hooked up with Kye in Austin, they would put no pressure on him to return. If he didn't want to be a part of their lives, they would just have to find a way to move on without him.

Ian shot her a warning glance. She nodded, mouthing the words, "I know," toward him. She kept her voice casual. "So, what time does your band go on?"

"We go on at nine. I'll let you know how it goes."

Cassidy heard someone calling Kye's name, a female someone. That voice was like cold water squirting through her veins. Had it happened just that fast? Were Ian and she already relegated to fond memories? She stiffened, biting her lip to keep from demanding who the hell that was.

"I have to go, love." Kye's tone was airy. "Rehearsal. I'll call again tomorrow."

Cassidy relayed his side of the conversation to Ian. "Bradley's," he mused. "Feel like going to a club tonight?"

C3

They were checked in at the B&B by three o'clock. The room they'd been given was charming, if cluttered, with a large, high, four-poster bed and old-fashioned mahogany furniture. The walls were papered in an intricate floral pattern, and the bureau and little tables set around the room were covered with knick-knacks resting on lace doilies. There was a large wardrobe in one corner, in lieu of a closet. Except for the fact it was spotlessly clean, the room looked like it had been decorated in the Victorian era and left untouched since.

They dropped their things and tested out the bed. The mattress, happily, wasn't from the turn of the century. It was new and firm. Ian lay back against a high stack of plump pillows and held out his arms. "Come here, you. Your gorgeous legs were driving me crazy the whole drive up here."

Cassidy laughed. She was wearing shorts and a sleeveless blouse. As they had driven, Ian's hand had often strayed to her bare thigh, stroking the skin, the fingers sometimes brushing perilously close to her crotch. "Concentrate on the road," she'd giggled at one point, noting the hard-on in his jeans.

She lay down beside him and he took her into his arms. They kissed for a while but eventually fell apart, lying side by side and staring up at the ceiling. Ian said aloud what she was thinking. "Do you think he'll be glad to see us?"

Too restless for lovemaking, they decided to take a walk by the lake. The actual temperature, at ninety, was higher than Houston's eighty-eight, but it felt markedly cooler without the humidity. Taking the advice of their hostess, they walked to a small marina located not far from the house where they were staying.

On the dock next to a small sailboat with a bright yellow striped sail stood a man with long gray hair pulled back in a ponytail and leathery tan skin. He waved toward them. "Would you like a tour of the lake?"

A neatly painted sign read, Rick's Sailboat Tours. The price seemed reasonable for an hour on the water and they both agreed it would be fun. Not only that, it would help to pass the time while they waited for nightfall.

The breeze on the water felt wonderful. Rick even had sunscreen handy, which was a good thing for Cassidy, who went from pale to burned, never quite arriving at tan along the way.

"Instead of a tour, do you think we could just sail out to the middle of the water and drift a little?" Cassidy turned to Ian. "That would be so peaceful. We don't really care about who owns what fancy homes along the shore, do we?"

"We do not," he answered with a grin. The guide was amenable, as long as he got paid. Once he had the boat out in the middle of the placid, glittering lake, Rick lowered the sail and dropped an anchor. The boat bobbed on the water. Cassidy leaned back and closed her eyes. The warm sun and the cool breeze, combined with the lulling movement of the boat, sent her into a near-doze.

Ian and the sailor were murmuring near her. She could almost imagine it was Kye, instead of a stranger, in the boat with them. It would be fun—just the three of them adrift, with no one around to observe them. She imagined herself, stretched out naked between them, their firm, masculine hands roaming over her body, touching her breasts, spreading her legs...

The sun was warm on her skin. She tried to move, but the sunlight itself seemed to carry weight. She couldn't even lift a finger. Even her eyes were sealed fast, the lids heavy. She was aware of the presence of her two lovers, though she was powerless to communicate. It was as if she were under some kind of magic spell. She knew the spell could only be broken if both of them made love to her at the same time, but she was powerless to tell them.

Fruitlessly they tried to revive her, calling her name, stroking her body, even finally slapping her face and shaking her shoulders. Though Cassidy was conscious, she couldn't respond or move a muscle. She was limp as a rag doll in their arms.

"It's no use," she heard Ian say, his voice defeated. "We've lost her. We've lost our Cassidy."

"Ach, no." Kye's thick, delightful brogue was like music to Cassidy's ears. "There has to be something we haven't tried." Strong arms scooped her up and settled her on his lap. She felt his warm skin against hers and realized he too was naked. His hard cock poked between her ass cheeks.

The head of his cock was pressing against her nether opening. As if she weighed nothing, he held her up, lowering her body onto his cock. It slipped in easily and didn't hurt at all. In fact it was wonderful. She moaned her approval and tried to move against him.

"Hey." Ian's voice floated excitedly near her. "She moved. And she made a sound. Whatever you're doing, it's working."

"It's working, but it's not enough," Kye answered. His cock was now buried deep in her ass. He swiveled beneath her, sending spirals of pleasure directly to her moistening pussy.

Again she moaned, or tried to. "She needs more. She needs us both. Come here, Ian. Kneel in front of us. Yes, that's it."

Ian's arms wrapped around her from the front, his warm,

sweet breath on her cheek as he spread her legs wide. She felt the tip of his cock at her pussy. He moved forward, entering her, filling her. She could actually feel each man's cock rubbing against the thin wall of membrane that separated them inside her.

As they moved, her body seemed to fill with a buttery light. She moaned her pleasure and this time the sound was audible, even loud. "It's working," Ian cried. "This is what she needed. She needed both of us. Don't you see, Kye? She needs us both."

"Yes," Cassidy whispered, opening her eyes and reaching for Ian. She could speak. She could move. The spell was broken. Together both men had set her free.

"Cassidy. Oh, Cassidy. Cassidy, my darling. Cassidy…"

Cassidy opened her eyes. Ian's face was just inches from hers. "Cassidy, wake up. Cassidy." She jerked away, startled and confused. Rick was watching them with a curious expression. Still caught in the throes of her dream, Cassidy, who was leaning back against the bow, legs akimbo, for a horrible moment thought she was stark naked.

She sat abruptly and slammed her legs together. With relief she saw she was fully clothed, if a little disheveled. "I—I fell asleep."

"No kidding." Ian grinned. "I've been calling your name for like fifty seconds. I could tell you were dreaming."

"What do you mean?" Cassidy wished Rick wasn't sitting so close. He could obviously hear every word they were saying.

"You kept twitching and sighing. And your eyes were moving—you know, that rapid eye movement thing. And," he leaned close, whispering in her ear, "your nipples were erect. I bet the dream was a good one. I hope I was in it."

"You were." She knew she was blushing. Her panties were soaked, and not from sweat. "I'll tell you all about it." She glanced toward Rick. "Later."

CR

Bradley's was located on Fifth Street in the warehouse district of downtown Austin. It had been easy to find and was apparently quite a popular venue, as the parking lot was packed, with people spilling out of the doors of the large club, leaning against the walls outside smoking cigarettes and laughing.

Ian and Cassidy ended up parking in a bank parking lot about a block down from the place. A large sign at the entrance read: *Pop Rocks—9:00—Two Nights Only.* Cassidy flipped open her cell phone—it was 8:20. As they pushed their way into the crowded room, Ian remarked, "We should have gotten here earlier. I don't think there's an empty table in the place."

It did appear to be standing room only. Most of the people in the room looked to be in their twenties and thirties, dressed in everything from jeans and cowboy boots to silk and high heels. The atmosphere was carnival-like, the air filled with expectation. Bluegrass was blaring over the loudspeakers. The large stage was set up with the band's equipment, and a young man in straight-leg black jeans and cowboy boots was tinkering with knobs at a soundboard off to the side and positioning microphones.

Cass and Ian made their way to the bar and ordered mugs of beer. "He might be in here already." Ian scanned the crowd. They had decided they would watch the set first, before trying to approach him. Hopefully he would be glad to see them.

Though the air conditioning was blasting from large vents in the ceiling, the room was warm with so many people. Cassidy lifted her hair and coiled it on her head, trying to get a breeze on the back of her neck. She was glad she'd worn a light sundress but wished she hadn't opted for the very cute but not very comfortable strappy sandals.

Ian was dressed in jeans and a dark blue T-shirt that offset his blond hair and golden brown eyes. She noticed quite a few women and even a few men glancing his way with barely concealed lust. Proprietarily she linked her arm in his.

"Hey, there's a table," he announced, pulling her along toward a corner of the room. The small table was cluttered with empty glasses and lipstick-stained napkins, but the seats were vacant. They sat down, turning toward the stage.

"Look." Cassidy pointed excitedly. From a small door at the back of the stage, three guys entered. One of them was the one who had been on the stage before. Of medium height, he had long dark hair and a scraggly beard. He looked about eighteen to Cassidy, who suddenly felt old. He sat at the keyboard and played a few notes, barely audible over the blast of music from the speakers.

The tallest of the three, with a shock of bright orange hair of a color not found in nature, made his way over to the drum kit. The third, a good-looking guy with shaggy dark blond hair and tattoos covering his arms, walked over to the guitar stand and lifted one of the instruments.

He looked out toward the audience and held up a guitar cable, a question on his face. Cassidy followed his gaze and saw there was a large, balding man off to the side down on the floor of the club. He sat behind a large, complicated-looking soundboard with dozens of knobs and buttons. He nodded and the guy on stage plugged in.

"Where's Kye?" Cassidy shifted impatiently in her seat.

"I think they're just doing a sound check," Ian offered. He put his hand on her arm and smiled. "Relax. You want another beer?"

"Okay." She remained at the table while Ian headed through the throng to procure two more beers. She watched the guys on the stage. No one else seemed to be paying them the slightest attention. Music continued to blare from the loudspeakers and talk and laughter bubbled around her.

The stage door opened again and there he was. Kye McClellan, as breathtakingly handsome as the first time she'd laid eyes on him back at Jim's Place. Her heart skipped a beat and tears popped into her eyes. God, she missed him.

She watched as he lifted the guitar she now recognized as his from the stand. The band was tuning, getting ready. They would be going on in a few minutes. She had an incredible urge to run up to the stage and call his name. He would extend his hand to her, pulling her up into his arms. While he held her tight, he would whisper into her hair how much he had missed her, what a terrible mistake he'd made in leaving...

Ian startled her with his return, setting a cold, sweating mug of beer down in front of her. "Oh." His gaze followed hers. "He's up there. Wow. He looks like a star, doesn't he?" Kye was dressed all in black, the cotton of his T-shirt and jeans molding to his sculpted body like a second skin. His dark hair was tousled and sexy looking, falling over his eyes. "Compared to those rug rats, he looks like he's in the wrong band, like he's sitting in with a bunch of kids."

"I guess that's what he's doing," Cassidy agreed. "Though I've been overhearing conversations about them. Apparently they're pretty good. I guess this crowd speaks for itself too. I don't think they could fit anyone else in here."

"Yeah. I almost want to go up there and tell him we're here. But I think it's better if we wait, don't you?"

"Yeah." Neither said aloud what Cassidy knew they were both thinking. There was a chance he *wouldn't* be glad to see them. He might feel like they were checking up on him— invading his space. Neither wanted to take that chance. They would wait and see, after the show.

The stage door opened yet again and this time a young woman came out. She had long, very straight, bright yellow-blonde hair and way too much eye makeup for Cassidy's taste. She wore a tiny vest that revealed more than it covered and a skirt of flowing, brightly patterned cotton. Her feet were bare.

Instead of moving toward an instrument to tune, she walked straight toward Kye, draping herself over him from behind. He turned back toward her and she took his face in her hands and kissed him square on the mouth.

"What the—?" Before she realized what she was doing, Cassidy stood. Ian put his hand on her arm, pulling her back down.

"Cass, sit down. It doesn't have to mean anything. All those musicians are like that. It's just for show."

Cassidy sat, desperately wanting to believe Ian. Kye had been gone less than a week. Could he really have already hooked up with someone new? Ian read her mind. "Don't leap to conclusions, Cass."

They both watched as the girl swung herself in front of Kye and wrapped herself around him. Cassidy clenched her fists and took a deep breath, trying to calm herself. How she wanted to be that girl, wrapped around that gorgeous man. Had it really been only a week since he had held *her* in his arms, whispering sweet things in his wonderful brogue as he made love to her?

They watched as Kye put his hands on the girl's arms and pushed her away with a shake of his head and what looked to Cassidy like a sardonic smile. She took some comfort from this, but not much.

"See, he's pushing her away. I wouldn't worry too much about that little scene. I bet she's doing it for the audience. I just don't see Kye with a kid like that. If anything, she's probably just got a crush and he's too gracious to outright reject her."

Cassidy tried to take hope from Ian's words. "You really believe that?"

He looked away. "I don't know." The hurt was palpable in his voice.

The music was good, edgy and soulful. Kye's guitar breaks were amazing, even to Cassidy, who didn't know that much about it. Every time he finished a lead, the audience burst into spontaneous applause, which filled her with pride, as if she had something to do with it, to do with him...

"Man, he's really good, huh? I mean, I knew he was good from his noodling around at home, but this is like professional stuff, right?" Ian too had the proud look of a parent or a spouse. In a more subdued tone, he added, "Maybe this is what he should be doing. Maybe the jewelry business and playing house with us was just something to pass the time, something to do along the way."

Cassidy's heart sank at these words, but she couldn't deny their validity. While he was up on stage playing, his face was suffused with a kind of glow. He seemed utterly absorbed in what he was doing, at one with his music, transported to a different plane of existence. But, she told herself, refusing to give up hope, he had that same expression on the porch, strumming his guitar for no one but them.

When the set was over, the audience roared for an encore. The young woman, who had introduced herself to the audience earlier as Summer, took the opportunity to pull Kye to her and again kiss him on the mouth while the audience cheered.

As the band settled back in for another song, Ian turned to Cassidy. "Maybe this isn't the right time?"

Cassidy, her heart breaking, had to agree. She hadn't expected the place to be so big and so crowded. She'd envisioned something more along the lines of a quiet coffeehouse with a few tables placed around a small stage.

This place was so impersonal. And Kye would no doubt be surrounded by fans the minute the set was over, that is, if the band didn't just file off the stage through that little back door. This had been a mistake. Or maybe it was the wakeup call they both needed—Kye was moving on. He was ready for something new.

It wasn't like he hadn't warned them from the beginning. He was a traveling man. A rambling gypsy always out for the new experience, like that song he'd used to sing so beautifully on their front porch. He'd taken whatever it was he'd wanted from them, and if he left them with broken hearts, that was their problem.

That didn't make it hurt any less. "It isn't *fair*," she blurted.

"I don't guess it's about fair," Ian responded sadly. They stood and Ian dropped a few bills on the table for the harried waitress who had cleared their table a while earlier and brought them a bowl of roasted peanuts.

Back in their cozy, romantic bedroom on the lake, Ian took Cassidy into his arms and kissed her, long and deep. "I love you, Cassidy Luke. No matter what happens or doesn't happen with Kye, I hope you know that."

She looked into his eyes, which were both sad and full of love. "I love you too, Ian Tanner. With or without Kye, I love you. I always have."

They fell together to the bed, pulling each other's clothing from their bodies. Ian's hands roamed greedily over her skin. She sensed his desperation, which mirrored her own. They were hungry, not only for each other, but for the closeness, the healing that lovemaking could lend them. For those few moments, lost in each other's arms, the world would be put on hold. No decisions to be made, no hard truths to face.

Ian slipped his fingers between Cassidy's legs as he kissed her neck. Despite her sadness, perhaps partially because of it, she clung to him, aching to feel his girth inside her.

She pulled him close, reaching down to guide his cock into her. She moaned, clinging tight. Wrapping her arms and legs around him, she pulled him closer, taking him as deep as she could. He held her tight, his body still, as if savoring the wet heat of her. It felt good. If only they could just stay like this, bodies joined like perfectly designed pieces of a jigsaw puzzle, all thoughts pushed aside by the raw physical pleasure of the connection.

He began to swivel inside her, causing her to shudder and arch up against him. They moved together in a steady, pulsing rhythm, punctuated with their sighs and moans of pleasure.

Bit by bit the world fell away—the aching knowledge Kye was only a few miles away but might as well be across the world, the image of that blonde girl wrapping herself around him like she owned him, the lingering memory of her dream—of Kye and Ian inside her, holding her, breaking the spell that had somehow kept her at a distance from the world until the moment the three of them joined.

As Ian made love to her, filling her, kissing her face and neck, his warm, heavy weight over her, the switches operating overtime in her brain clicked off one by one.

"Yes, yes," she whispered urgently. The orgasm that rolled over her came suddenly, catching her by surprise. She held on to Ian, clinging to him as if she might be swept away by its power.

A moment later Ian stiffened and then ejaculated, thrusting in several long spurts of passion before falling limply against her. Their hearts were thudding, one against the other. She was unable to distinguish whose beat was whose.

They lay tangled in a tight embrace, sweat drying, breath slowing. Eventually Ian unwrapped himself from her and fell back beside her. Though he didn't say anything, Cassidy knew

171

he was thinking about Kye, about how it would have been if he'd been with them.

In fact, Kye was so present in both their thoughts, it was as if he were in the room with them, watching, smiling at them with that dimpled grin, his head cocked to the side, reading their minds and hearts as he so often seemed to.

Unable to stand it, she blurted, "You're thinking about him too, huh?"

"Yeah."

They were silent again. Cassidy became aware of the ticking of the antique clock on the bureau. The room was bathed in moonlight, blanketed in silvered shadow. Ian's voice was soft but emphatic. "I think we need to talk to him. We need to be direct about this. It's like with us, with any relationship. Communication is the key. We haven't confronted him about any of this. We just let him go with barely a protest. Maybe he thinks *we're* the ones who didn't want him around. Maybe he thinks he's doing us a favor."

"How could he think that? He *knows* how much we love him," Cassidy protested.

"Does he? We think he overheard that conversation, remember? When I was saying I wanted more time with you." Ian drew his hand over his eyes. "Man, what an idiot I was. I realize that now. Kye is the best thing that ever happened to us. He didn't pull us apart, he brought us together. He's, I don't know, the glue that holds us together. We're better as a couple with him in our lives." Ian sounded surprised at his own words.

He went on. "Maybe his going was a good thing for us. I mean, it's really crystallized how we feel. Put it into perspective." He sat up and turned to her, his eyes blazing with intensity. "I want him in our lives, Cass. I want Kye to be part of what we mean when we say 'we'. Do you want that too?"

Cassidy nodded. "I do want that. More than anything."

"Okay then, now we just have to let Kye know. What he does with the information, well—that's up to him."

Chapter Thirteen

"Kye, Henry *Cohen* is here. He's with *Black Star.* He *loved* our set. He wants to meet you. He's coming this way. Oh my God, oh my God, oh my *God.*" Summer gripped Kye's arm so hard her long nails dug into the skin. Turning from the bar, where he was nursing his second pint of Guinness Stout, he raised his eyebrows.

"And just who is Henry Cohen and what is Black Star?"

Summer looked stunned. "You don't know the Black Star label? Only *the* cutting-edge label for the hottest of Austin's new bands. You get a contract with them, you have made it. We're talking gigs all over Texas, maybe a video on MTV, your CD placed in stores all over the country, on the Internet, on I-Tunes. This is serious, Kye. *Serious.*"

"I'm happy for you, Summer. I'm happy for the band. But I'm not part of the band. I'm just sitting in for a night or two. I mean, it was fun and all but—"

"No." She cut him off abruptly. "You don't get it. As far as Henry Cohen is concerned, you're part of the band. Shit, you heard the audience. They went nuts for your playing. Not to mention your look, all in black, so absorbed in the music it was like you were making love onstage to your guitar. I doubt Cohen would have bothered with us if it weren't for you up there. You *are* part of the band. Please, don't ruin this break for us. Just listen to the guy. We can talk details later. *Please.*"

Before he could answer, a short, balding man approached them. He was carrying a large cotton handkerchief, which he wiped over the top of his perspiring head. He was wearing a white silk suit, a black T-shirt beneath the jacket and pointy-toed cowboy boots of bright red elaborately stenciled leather. A long black onyx earring dangled from one lobe. Kye's initial impression was, no matter how famous or important in the Austin music scene this guy might be, he was trying way too hard.

Summer cast Kye a last pleading look and then turned a sunny smile on Cohen. "Mr. Cohen, this is Kye McClellan. He couldn't *wait* to meet you."

Kye bit back a smile at this lie and shook Cohen's plump, moist hand. When Cohen finished an enthusiastic pumping, Kye resisted the urge to wipe his hand on his napkin, instead shoving it into his back pocket.

Cohen's voice was booming and deep, too big for such a small man. "Summer tells me you're the newest addition to the band. What I want to know is where in the hell you've been hiding yourself. Your guitar work is reminiscent of Richard Thompson. The way you weave those chords together, it's really something to hear. You're obviously a professional musician, so where do you play? Why aren't you on my radar? I know everyone in this town, Mr. McClellan. *Everyone.*"

Kye couldn't help but be pleased by the comparison to Richard Thompson, who was, in his opinion, the best guitarist on the planet. In fact, he'd been heavily influenced by Thompson's style, though of course he could never hold a candle to the man's genius.

"I'm not from around here," he responded. "In fact, I'm not really a member—"

"He's from Scotland," Summer burst out, her nails again digging into his arm. "Only recently relocated."

"That accent. It's *terrific.* It will add to the appeal of the band. Give you a more international flavor. Now, I'm not in the position at the moment to offer a contract on the spot, but I assume y'all have a CD?" When Summer nodded enthusiastically, Cohen continued. "Good, good." He reached into his jacket and pulled out a slim gold card case. From it he extracted a business card and held it out toward Kye. Summer snatched it.

"Send me a CD, whatever you've got. We'll do a meeting. Maybe sometime next week."

"Oh, thank you, Mr. Cohen," Summer gushed, transferring her hand from Kye's arm to his. "We'll definitely be in touch."

℃

Kye lay on Summer's futon sofa, exhausted but wide-eyed. What a long, strange night it had been. They'd worked hard all day preparing for the gig. He hadn't expected Bradley's to be such a large place, nor had he expected the capacity crowd.

A part of him was glad to be there, but another part of him, the aching, lonely part, just wanted to go back home to Cassidy and Ian. Still, he had to admit, the actual performance had been a serious high. They'd come together as a group in a way they hadn't in rehearsal.

He had slipped into that zone where he actually became one with his instrument. He didn't know how to describe it to a non-musician. The closest he could come was to compare it to really good sex. The connection, when it was achieved, was as powerful as any orgasm.

Mostly he'd ignored the crowd, losing himself in the sound, as he always did. For him, it wasn't about performing for an audience so much as making music. He was as happy doing it on the porch by himself as in front of a bunch of people.

If only Cass and Ian had been there. It was funny, he'd imagined for a moment he'd seen them toward the end of the evening. At least Cassidy, her ginger-red hair shining toward the back of the room. When he'd looked again, she, or whoever it was, because of course it couldn't have been her, was gone.

He should have invited them to come up to Austin for the show. Maybe he would invite them up if he played with the band the next night. He hadn't committed one way or the other, unable to make up his mind what he should do.

But would they want to come? He knew they were angry with him for just taking off like he'd done. But were they also relieved to have him gone? He knew they needed to talk, the three of them, and about more than accounts receivable and cash flow.

Jesus, he was lonely. The room was warm, the small air conditioner lodged in one window of the living room not up to the job. Pushing the sheet down, he turned on his side, closing his eyes. Again Summer had invited him to her bed, and again he'd refused. Now he almost wished he hadn't. He could use the comfort of someone beside him, someone to hold, someone to kiss, someone to keep the loneliness at bay, at least until morning.

He must have dozed because when he awoke she was there behind him, nestled against his back, her soft breasts pressing against him. He was only half-awake. "Cassidy," he murmured under his breath, turning toward her.

The room was dark and still. The girl climbed up over him, straddling his hips with strong, bare thighs. He started to speak but she put her finger to his lips. "Shh," she whispered. "It's a dream. Just a dream."

He closed his eyes, almost believing it, though this girl's scent was different, patchouli and vanilla, instead of Cassidy's fresh rain and honeysuckle. She rubbed herself over his erect shaft. It felt nice. If this was a dream, it was a good one. But when her hand encircled his shaft and gripped it hard, he came fully awake.

He pulled himself up, pushing her from him. "No. Stop it. This isn't right."

The naked girl tumbled away from him, nearly falling off the futon. "Hey." Her voice was petulant, even angry. "Don't pretend you don't want me. I saw the way you stared at my tits during rehearsal. Come on. No harm. Just two people taking a little pleasure in the dark."

He groped for the reading lamp by the sofa and flicked it on. Summer's eye makeup had been inexpertly removed, leaving a black smudge beneath each eye. She looked even younger than before, like a little girl who had gotten into Mommy's makeup.

What the hell was he doing here? How had it come to this? She was watching him, her arms wrapped around her knees, her golden hair falling in a smooth sheet over one side of her pretty face, her expression one of challenge. She wasn't, he was sure, used to being turned down by a man.

"Summer, love. It's not that I don't find you attractive. You're a lovely girl. We've known each other all of two days. And this may sound like a cliché, but my heart belongs to another. Sometimes you need to accept it when a person says no. Okay?"

Her face darkened and she scowled. He half expected her to demand he pack his things and leave at once. *Hell hath no fury like a woman scorned...* Then he remembered she needed him, or thought she did, for her recording contract.

She apparently remembered this too, for she smiled, though her eyes were flat. "What*ever*." Her inflection further convinced him she was definitely closer to eighteen than her alleged twenty-four. "I wasn't really in the mood anyway."

She flounced out of the room and he lay back down, feeling, if possible, even lonelier than before.

CⳫ

The sky outside lightened, moving from inky black to gray to a pale, eggshell blue streaked with thin white clouds. After Summer returned to her bedroom, Kye lay awake, staring at that patch of sky, his mind wandering over everything from his childhood in Scotland, his falling out with his father over the business, his years of traveling across the globe, always searching, searching, though until now he'd never quite known for what.

He'd never really figured he was looking for love. For a while he'd thought he might like to be a professional musician, but soon recognized he wasn't cut out for the grind. He didn't care enough about getting the gig, about making it. He also didn't like the hassle of trying to find a band, of coordinating for rehearsals and dealing with egos.

He'd always thought of himself as a loner, passing through other people's lives, moving on when the time seemed right. Had he been fooling himself? What was he really running from?

He thought about Derek, who seemed determined to remain on a collision course with misery, unless he was derailed by those around him. He thought about Ian and Cassidy as he mused over every detail of their complicated relationship. Could two really open up enough to accept a third? Would he always, no matter how close the three of them became, feel like the odd man out?

Was that in itself reason enough not to try?

At five fifteen in the morning he rolled from the futon and pulled it into its upright position, folding the sheet and blanket

Summer had provided him and leaving them in a neat pile. He pulled on his clothes, thinking he'd like to shower, but too determined to move forward with his plans to take the time. Nor did he want to risk waking the sleeping girl in the next room.

He rummaged through the piles of papers and bills on the kitchen counter, finding an empty envelope and a pen. With a pang of guilt that was overridden by a rising excitement, he sat down to write.

Dear Summer,

This note will find me gone. I'm going back to Houston, which I realize now is where I belong. I appreciate your hospitality in letting me crash at your place these last few days. Thanks for the chance to perform with your band. You guys have great potential and I know you'll go far. I wish you and the band the very best of luck.

He signed the note and put it on top of the folded bedding. Grabbing his duffel, laptop bag and guitar, he slipped quietly out the door.

03

By eight o'clock that morning he was back in Houston. Coasting into the driveway of their old Victorian house, it seemed as if he'd been gone for months instead of days. Stiffly he climbed off the motorcycle, unbuckling the straps that held his guitar to his back with a sigh of relief.

His heart was fluttering with nervous anticipation. He couldn't wait to see them again, to wrap them both in his arms, to announce he'd come home. Yes, home. For the first time in his adult life he felt truly at home.

He took off the helmet and shook out his hair. He inhaled a deep lungful of fresh morning air. The day was drier than usual for Houston in summer, an almost-cool breeze blowing through his hair. The huge old mimosa tree had dropped most of its fat, fragrant pink blossoms onto the driveway. Their lush scent permeated the air.

That was when he noticed their car wasn't in the driveway. A wave of disappointment washed over him. He'd been counting on arriving early enough to be there in the kitchen, breakfast cooking, when they woke up.

He knew things couldn't just pick up where they'd left off—they'd have to talk things through and really assess where they were in the relationship. But at least they could do it over a good hearty breakfast.

He paused at the front door, for a second wondering if he should knock or just walk in. He turned the knob—the door was locked. They never locked it when someone was at home. Using his key, he opened the door and stepped inside.

The house was oddly quiet. He peered across the studio, half-expecting to find Ian bent over his worktable. Cassidy might have just gone out to run an errand or drop off an order to a customer.

But the studio was empty. So were the dining room, the kitchen and the sunroom beyond. He returned to the studio and, just in case, called up the stairs but there was no answer. Then he noticed the pile of mail on the floor in front of the mail slot in the door. He picked it up, mechanically sorting through bills and junk mail. There was a newspaper in the pile.

Ian always grabbed the paper first thing. He liked to read it with his breakfast. That must mean they'd been gone since at least the night before, as the paper was always delivered by seven in the morning.

Where had they gone? Why hadn't they told him they were leaving? What was going on?

Why should they tell you, a voice in his head said. *You're the one who left them, with vague plans of when you might return. Why shouldn't they do what they want? It's not like they owe you an explanation.*

"Aye, they do," he said out loud. "I run their business. They need to let me know when they've abandoned their posts. Very irresponsible, just to run off like that." He stopped and shut his mouth. Jesus, had the day really come when he was holding conversations with himself, like some lonely, doddering old man? And *he'd* run off, hadn't he? Sure, he'd kept in touch by laptop and phone, but who was to say they couldn't do the same? Still, he couldn't imagine Ian away from his worktable for very long.

He climbed the stairs and stopped at their bedroom. The door was ajar, the bed inside empty and neatly made. He entered the room and sat heavily on the bed. It hadn't occurred to him they might not be here. He'd played out the various ways his return might be received, but their absence had never been part of the possible scenarios. The half-formed fantasies he'd been harboring of a joyful reunion dissipated like smoke curling over his shoulder.

He touched his cell phone through the pocket of his jeans. Reaching in, he pulled it out and flipped it open. It was fully charged and there were no missed calls.

He glanced at the door. Cassidy's purse, which usually hung on the knob, wasn't there. Ian's watch was missing from the pewter bowl on their bureau where he usually kept it. He resisted a sudden urge to riffle through their bureau to try to figure out what they'd packed.

With a sigh he re-pocketed his phone and lay back against the bed. He could call them and find out where they were, but he didn't want to. They'd ruined his plans of the grand homecoming and though he knew it was childish, he was irritated with them.

He closed his eyes, which felt gritty from the nearly three

hours on the open road on his motorcycle. What he needed was a hot shower and a hot cup of coffee. He would get up and do that, in just a moment...just a moment.

Lying there, the exhausting pace of the last few days, coupled with next to no sleep the night before, caught up with him all at once. It pinned him to the mattress so he could barely move. His chest felt like someone had put one of those dentist's weighted vests over it, the kind they use to take x-rays, only thirty kilos heavier.

With no choice in the matter, he gave in to the sleep rolling over him like a tide, dragging him down into a dreamless torpor.

CB

"This is silly. We should just call him." They were sitting at the large round table in the dining room at the B&B. Their hostess was plying them with a huge assortment of breakfast foods. Two other couples were at the table as well, making small talk and waxing enthusiastic about the accommodations.

Cassidy and Ian had been talking quietly to each other, trying to decide what to do. "The sign said his band's going to be playing again tonight. Maybe we should just wait and show up again," Cassidy suggested.

"I don't know," Ian answered. "I don't want him to think we were spying on him. I mean, it's bound to come out we were there last night too. Surely he'd want to know why we didn't approach him then."

"We didn't approach him because that bimbo slut was climbing all over him, that's why," Cassidy snapped quite uncharacteristically.

Ian grinned, amused. This was a new side of Cassidy. Still, he couldn't deny a niggling sense of jealousy as well. That girl, while young, was beautiful and had a great voice. Maybe Kye found her more compelling, more exotic, than the two of them. Or maybe he was ready for something new. What they'd mistaken for a growing love was simply lust that had run its course.

No. Even as this thought percolated through his brain, he rejected it. He knew the truth. He just had to face it. They all did.

"You know what?" he announced with sudden conviction. "This is stupid. We're all dancing around each other like we're strangers. Damn it, we *love* Kye. We want him back. What had seemed so easy, so right, has suddenly become this huge thing between us. This stumbling block. Instead of talking it through like adults, we just let him go like it was nothing. We let the best thing ever to happen to us as a couple just slip through our hands. So I blame us for that. I blame myself, especially. But also, I blame Kye."

Ian knew he was speaking rapidly. He tried to slow himself down, to get his feelings under control. "It's funny too, because Kye's the one who told me I needed to learn to communicate better. But it seems to me he's done a pretty piss-poor job this time around. What were his words? He said he needed some time to figure things out. What things? I'm pretty damn sure those things involve us, so why not include us in the figuring? Is he holding back some deep dark secret? Is he married with a family back in Scotland?"

Cassidy laughed, shaking her head. "Kye married? I don't think so."

"No, me neither. But see, that's the point. We don't *know*. For all the great stories he tells about his travels, when did he ever really open up about himself? You told him everything about us, I know you did. I did too. He's so easy to talk to. He never judged. He always offered great advice. But when did he ever share his own weaknesses and fears? What about this

Derek guy? We know next to nothing about him. We know next to nothing about why he left Scotland, other than vague discussion about disagreeing with his father about how to run a business.

"As much as I love Kye, and I do, I'm not saying otherwise, what do we really know about him?"

Cassidy was silent. Finally she said, "You're right. But we can't make him tell us his life story. We can't *command* that he open up to us. We have to give him the space and time to feel comfortable enough to come to that on his own. We have to be his safe place. The place he can finally come home to. Is that what you want, Ian? Are you really ready for that?"

Ian looked into Cassidy's beautiful green eyes. Was she really asking him? Would she accept it if he said he wasn't? If he admitted he wanted only her in his life—that there was no room for a third? He took a step back in his mind, searching it to give as honest an answer as he could.

He knew he loved Cassidy and yes, was *in* love with her, whether or not Kye had a permanent place in their lives. But these past days apart from him had really helped him see how much a part of their lives Kye had already become. Ian had found a place for them both in his heart, and he hated the emptiness Kye had caused by leaving them so abruptly. Ian refused to consider what they would do if Kye didn't come back. "Yes, yes I am. Let's call him, Cassidy. Let's ask him to come home."

Chapter Fourteen

Something was vibrating in Kye's pocket. At first he wrapped it up into his dreams, assigning it to the rumble of the motorcycle engine beneath him. He was on a long, straight highway, racing as fast as he could toward something he was trying desperately to reach, but whenever he came close, it receded.

He opened his eyes, for a moment not sure where he was. The phone vibrated again and hurriedly he shoved his hand into his pocket and withdrew it. *C. Luke*, read the caller ID.

"Hello? Cassidy?"

"Kye?"

"Cassidy, where are you?"

"Funny you should ask." She gave a small embarrassed laugh. He sat up against the headboard, his gut clenching. "We're right near you, actually. We're just outside of Austin, at a quaint bed and breakfast."

"Outside of *Austin*? Ian's with you?"

"Sure he's with me. Where else would he be?"

"I don't know. What're you doing there?"

"Well, we kind of thought it would be nice to get away a little. You know, we haven't had a break really since the startup of the business. And we thought we might come see you? Maybe catch your show tonight?"

Kye started to laugh. What a comedy of errors. Here he'd left at the crack of dawn, so eager to see them, so eager to reunite, and they in turn had come to see him. Yet something wasn't quite right. What was it? He glanced at his watch. It was a little after eleven. He'd slept like the dead for three straight hours. But they'd been gone when he'd arrived. Long gone.

"Wait a minute. Let me get this straight. How long have you been in Austin? I know you've been there at least since yesterday." He didn't explain how he knew and Cassidy didn't ask.

Cassidy sounded guilty, though he didn't yet know of what. "Yes, you're right. We arrived in Austin early yesterday afternoon, actually. But we didn't want to bother you. I mean, it's obvious you have something going on with the girl on stage and—oh." There was dead silence for several seconds as Kye took in the implications of what she'd just said.

"You were there? At Bradley's?" Kye tried to piece it together. He wasn't sure if he should be upset or happy. So he *had* seen Cassidy's lovely hair glinting in the distance when he'd been onstage. They'd been there but they hadn't approached him. Why?

"I don't understand," he finally said, while at the same time Cassidy blurted, "Damn. I'm making a mess of this. Here, talk to Ian."

A moment later Ian's voice came over the phone. "Kye? Listen, can we meet somewhere? We both miss you so much. That's why we're here. We want to see you. We need to talk. About a lot of things."

"Yes, yes, I guess we do," Kye agreed. "I miss you too. When I got here and found you gone—"

"Got where? Where are you?"

"I'm in Houston." He laughed hollowly. "I'm at the house. I came home to tell you this is where I belong."

Ian gave a startled laugh. Kye could hear him as he said to Cassidy, "Shit! He's at home! Can you believe that?" To Kye he said, "So I guess you aren't playing again tonight, huh? Why the sudden change of heart? It looked like you belonged up there."

"Why didn't you tell me you were there? I would have loved knowing you were in the audience."

"Oh, well. I don't know. The timing seemed off, somehow. I mean, we had kind of just shown up, after you'd been pretty adamant about needing some time to clear your head or whatever. It just didn't feel quite right to approach you, especially not after the way the singer in the band, Summer was it? I mean...it was obvious there was something between you..."

"No. No, no, no. Nothing at all but music." The image of Summer, naked and climbing over him in the dark, jutted into his mind. He shook it away, deeply relieved he'd rebuffed her, aware he'd been tempted, if just for a moment. He continued, "Even that was just a temporary thing. I enjoyed playing with the band for a lark, but that's not really my thing. I prefer making music by myself. I guess I'm a just a solo kind of guy." He paused, adding, "When it comes to making music, I mean. Not when it comes to relationships. I think I'm finally figuring that out now."

There was a silence. Absently he stroked the pillow, feeling the distance between them, wanting desperately to bridge it. "Come home. I'll be here waiting."

⋈

Kye was on the porch, working out a new, intricate riff that had come to him on the ride back from Austin. Glancing up, he saw their car pull into the drive. He stood, setting the guitar down in its velvet-lined case as he waited for them. He felt nervous, even awkward, knowing they'd been separated by far more than time.

Cassidy came hurtling toward him, throwing herself into his arms. He forgot his nerves as she wrapped herself around him. "Kye, oh Kye. We missed you so much. Don't run off and leave us ever again, you hear me?"

He laughed with sheer joy. Ian walked up the steps, moving with more caution. He stood at the top of the steps watching the two of them. Looking over Cassidy's head, Kye smiled. After a moment, Ian smiled back.

CB

It was too early for dinner but they were all a little hungry.

"Let me see what I can find in the—" Kye began.

Cassidy cut him off. "No, you sit down. Relax. I'll get it." It was one of the things she'd been ruminating over while he'd been gone. Because it was easy, because he was there, ready, willing and able, they'd abdicated more and more of the basic responsibilities of running the household to Kye. And while there was no dispute that he was the far better cook, it didn't mean they had to let him wait on them like some kind of servant. Though he'd never given any indication he resented it, Cassidy had made a personal vow to step up and act more like a grown woman who owned her own house.

The two men settled on the sofa. Ian had been mostly silent during the drive, and Cassidy knew he was girding himself for their talk. Kye was looking positively nervous, not something she was used to seeing in the relaxed, easygoing Scotsman.

Leaning down, she kissed each man on the cheek. "I'll be right back."

She moved around the kitchen, taking a block of Muenster cheese from the refrigerator and slicing it into thin wedges.

Arranging the cheese on a large ceramic platter, she added fresh tomato slices and some olives. She fanned some wheat crackers around the edges and stood back, relatively pleased with the arrangement. She put the platter on a large serving tray and pulled three bottles of beer from the refrigerator.

Kye appeared in the kitchen door. "Here, let me help you with that."

She let him carry the tray, following behind with the bottles. "Where's Ian?"

"Just ran up to wash his face. He'll be right down."

They placed the food on the coffee table in front of the sofa and sat. The easy joy Cassidy had felt upon first seeing Kye had been replaced, or at least augmented, by a certain lack of ease between them, or perhaps it was nervous anticipation. None of them were quite sure where they stood.

Ian came down the stairs and joined them on the sofa. "Nice spread." Ian automatically nodded toward Kye as he reached for a piece of cheese.

Kye took a cracker, adding cheese and tomato and topping it off with another cracker. "Courtesy of Cassidy." He popped the miniature sandwich into his mouth.

Ian looked surprised. He glanced at Cassidy. She grinned and shrugged. He took a long drink of his beer. Cassidy could tell he was gearing up. He continued. "It's funny how we assume things, isn't it? We made some assumptions about you, and you about us, and I think it's created some issues for us, some things we need to talk through."

"Look." Kye sounded defensive. "I know it was kind of sudden, my taking off like that. I just—I needed some time. Some time to figure things out."

"And did you?" Ian's voice was full of hurt. "Did you figure out it's scary to get really close to people, and then did you just decide it's okay to take off while you get your head on straight?

It's okay to just drop into our lives, become completely involved in every aspect of them, make us fall crazy in love with you and then just split the second you start feeling hemmed in? Did you give a second thought to who you were leaving behind and how it might affect us? Or did you forget all about that, once you found a new heart to break?"

"Ian," Cassidy warned.

Kye knit his brows and frowned. "*What?*" He sounded incredulous. Ian had gone too far. "A new heart to break? Are you talking about Summer? The girl in the band?"

"The very one," Ian asserted, crossing his arms. "You like to go on about what a free spirit you are. Well, I think that's a crock. Something to hide behind. The minute things get too intense, too vulnerable, too *real,* you take off."

"Now hold on right there." Kye stood abruptly, turning to face them. His cheeks were flushed and he was breathing hard. He took a deep breath and blew it out, obviously trying to calm down. When he spoke, his tone was calmer. "Not that I have to defend my actions, but I did not have sex with that girl." He shook his head as if the very idea was ludicrous.

"Look, I'm sorry. I really am. I know it was the act of a coward, the way I just hit the road like that." He sat back down between the two of them. "But regarding Summer, you're way off base. She's a kid. If you think I'd get involved with someone like that, you don't know me too well. Her flirtations were a reflex, I think. She only came on to me because I was there—I was someone new for her to conquer. When I refused her, I think that only made her want me more, not because she cared who I was, but because she wasn't used to being refused."

Cassidy and Ian were silent, watching him. Ian looked embarrassed for his own outburst, but determined to hold his ground. Cassidy believed Kye was telling the truth.

Leaning forward, his elbows on his knees, Kye dropped his

head into his hands. After a moment he looked up, his eyes nearly silver in the light, filled with a longing so palpable it made Cassidy ache for him, and for herself and for Ian.

"Listen. I didn't go to Austin to find someone new. I left because..." He pressed his lips together, as if it hurt to say the words. "Because I was scared."

He turned to Ian. "About what happened before I left. You know, when Cassidy was out with her girlfriends—"

"Forget it," Ian interjected, looking embarrassed.

"No, I can't. I wanted to apologize. I rebuffed you because of my own issues and insecurities. I was a real jerk that night. I'm sorry. I hope you can forgive me."

Ian nodded, his expression softening.

Kye continued. "What you said is true. I call myself a free spirit, but this last week away from you, away from the best thing ever to happen to me, made me realize I'm less of a free spirit, and more driven by the fear of getting too close to someone and then getting hurt. I'll be twenty-nine in a couple of weeks, and I've never been in a committed relationship that lasted longer than a few months.

"Look, I don't know exactly what we have between us." He sighed and Cassidy wanted to hug him, but knew he didn't want that right now. He clearly was determined to say what he had to say. She sat back and waited. Ian too, was watching him, his expression intense.

"Being with you, with the two of you, is like nothing I've ever experienced. I love being involved in your lives, in the business, in the running of this great old house. I love the unique nature of our relationship. There isn't even a word for it. I mean, you have couples and then what? A threesome? A ménage? Those terms have sexual meaning, sure, but they don't have the intimacy of the word *couple*. I left partially because of what I overheard. I didn't mean to eavesdrop, but you made it clear you two also needed your space, some time alone."

Cassidy glanced at Ian, who looked down. So he *had* overheard, as they'd suspected.

"I'm sorry," Ian began. "That was just me being—"

"Scared." Kye raised his eyebrows and smiled a small smile.

"Yeah," Ian admitted. "You're right. Scared of losing what I'd rediscovered with Cassidy. Of being overwhelmed by what was going on between the three of us." He shrugged. "I was feeling insecure, I guess."

"But that's not the only reason you left, is it, Kye?"

Kye turned to face Cassidy. "No. It wasn't. I left because I'm selfish. I didn't want to be the third wheel. I told myself I was moving on because that's what I do. I'm a wanderer. But when I got to Austin, all I wanted was to be home. With you. I realized something else. Even if that's all I can ever be for you, it's enough. Even if it's always going to be Cassidy and Ian, and Kye—a couple plus one, well, I'll take it.

"I told myself I had to go because I couldn't bear always wondering if I could ever be as close to the two of you as you are to each other. I came to realize over this past week that it doesn't matter. The love we each have for the others is unique and doesn't have to be quantified or divvied out in equal portions.

"I guess what I'm trying to say is, I want to be a part of your lives, however that shakes out. I'm tired of running. I'm ready to grow up. I'm ready to stay for as long as you'll have me."

Kye's mouth was dry. In the hours while waiting for their return he'd rehearsed any number of speeches, moving in his head from defensive, to pleading, to a feigned casualness he most certainly didn't feel. Finally he'd said to hell with it, pulled out his guitar and lost himself in his music.

Now he waited, his head bowed, his hands in his lap, for their decree. He sensed Cassidy's sympathy and yearning, which gave him hope. Ian was still the unknown. Ian, from whom he had run in the first place, stung by what he'd overheard, was at the moment in a position of power. The realization was disconcerting, as Kye was used to being the one in control.

Cassidy put her hand on his thigh and squeezed. He glanced toward her. Tears were in her eyes but she was smiling. Ian's hand dropped to his other thigh. He turned to face him. "Kye." Ian's voice cracked with emotion. "We'd like nothing better than if you'd stay for as long as your gypsy heart will allow."

He leaned forward, kissing Kye on the forehead, and Kye felt curiously as if he'd been blessed, a benediction bestowed on him by Ian. A weight he hadn't realized he'd been carrying somehow lifted with that kiss and he sat up straighter.

"Yes," Cassidy affirmed beside him. She stood and held out her hands toward the two men. Kye and Ian both rose from the sofa, each taking an offered hand. Without speaking, she led them through the room toward the stairs. Nimbly she leaped up a few steps and leaned down to kiss each one on the cheek. With an impish grin, she pulled her T-shirt over her head and tossed it toward the men.

Turning on her heel, she dashed up the stairs. "Last one up's a rotten egg," she called, laughing.

Ian turned to Kye with a grin. "That girl"—he shook his head in mock dismay—"always has only one thing on her mind."

Kye raised his eyebrows, aware of his rising erection. He glanced pointedly at the bulge swelling in Ian's jeans as well. "We could always stay down here and talk some more."

Ian nodded sagely and they stared at one another with serious, manly expressions for all of three seconds before they burst out laughing. Suddenly they were shoving and pushing each other, stumbling up the stairs as fast as they could, tearing off their shirts as they ran.

Cassidy was lying on the bed, wearing only a pair of black silky panties. Ian entered the room, pulling off his jeans and kicking them, along with his underwear, aside. With a laugh, he bounded onto the bed and turned toward Kye. "Come on. It's your bed too."

Kye felt an odd shyness, though his cock was straining hard at the sight of the handsome couple. Cassidy's breasts were sheer perfection, the rosy-pink nipples perking toward him. Her creamy skin looked soft as satin and he knew from his own experience that it was. His fingers actually itched with the desire to stroke that lovely flesh.

He turned toward Ian, drinking in the sight of his broad, smooth chest and hard cock rising from a nest of dark blond curls. After a diet of regular sex with these two gorgeous creatures, the self-imposed celibacy of the last week made him ache all the more. Hurriedly he stripped off his shorts and underwear, aching for both of them.

He moved into their waiting arms. They kissed for several minutes. Kye buried his head in Cassidy's luxurious hair, reveling in the sweet, familiar scent of her. When he could bear to let her go, he turned toward Ian.

The shyness between them downstairs was gone. Pulling back from a kiss, Kye licked a line down Ian's cheek and throat, tasting the salty tang of sweat, which mingled with his woodsy aftershave. Ian clutched Kye's cock and Kye groaned.

Kye tilted his head back toward Ian's face and they kissed again, tongues at first lazily exploring each other's mouths, becoming more insistent as they stroked each other's cocks. He turned to find Cassidy on his other side, watching them with shining eyes and parted lips. Eagerly he tasted her sweet mouth while Ian continued to massage his cock.

He sought her nipples, taking them one at a time into his mouth and suckling them. Ian moved behind him, spooning him, his hard shaft pressing between Kye's cheeks. Kye was like a kid in a candy store, one who couldn't decide which delectable treat to taste next. He rolled onto his back, extending his arms on either side to draw them both close.

As if they'd planned it beforehand, both Cassidy and Ian pulled away. Kye sat up, confused. He needed to feel their bare skin on his, their lips on his mouth, their bodies hard against his. "Hey...what?"

"Lie back." Cassidy's voice took on a sultry quality. "We want to take care of you." Ian nodded, pressing Kye back against the pillows. He complied with a happy sigh as Cassidy slid down to take his cock in her long, cool fingers. Warm lips closed over his shaft and Cassidy began to do amazing things with her tongue and the lightest grazing of her teeth. His eyes narrowed with pleasure and then fluttered shut. He groaned, surrendering himself to her skillful touch.

He was vaguely aware of Ian maneuvering nearby, reaching for the condoms they kept in the nightstand. He heard the familiar tear of the plastic wrapper. After several delicious minutes, Cassidy released his cock and sat back. He opened his eyes, watching as Ian, already similarly prepared, rolled a condom over his wet, hard cock.

Cassidy lay back on the pillows beside them. Her cheeks and chest were flushed, her eyes a vivid green and burning with lust. She didn't have to ask—he knew what she wanted.

Still not entirely sure of his role in this sexual dance between three, he turned to Ian, silently asking for direction. "She wants you. I want you. We both mean to have you." Ian nodded toward the lovely girl, who had let her long, slender legs fall open.

Kye got to his knees and moved between her thighs. Using his fingers, he opened her carefully. She moaned. "Yes."

Ian leaned close to her and whispered into her ear. She nodded and flashed a devilish smile in Kye's direction. Then she rolled over and lifted herself to her hands and knees.

Cassidy turned to him, her long, ginger hair falling in a sweep over her back. "Take me, Kye. And Ian will take you." Kye glanced at Ian, who nodded. Until this moment, he'd received Kye, but never penetrated him in turn. Kye could see the lust burning bright in his eyes.

Ian opened the tube of lubrication and smeared some over his cock. He squeezed a bit more on his fingers and stroked the head of Kye's cock, coating the condom that sheathed it. Kye shivered at his touch. He was on fire, desperate for Ian's hard cock, filling him while he filled Cassidy.

He was surprised to see his hands actually trembling with his barely contained desire. He used Cassidy's hips to steady himself, positioning his cock at her sex and rolling forward until he filled her. Cassidy moaned, pushing herself back against him. He swiveled in slow circles, reveling in her sensitive response. She shivered and sighed and he felt powerful, like a snake charmer, and she the cobra, at once mesmerized, tamed and ravished by his movements.

Ian positioned himself behind Kye, sandwiching him between the two. Ian's finger, gooey with lube, slipped into Kye's ass. After a moment, a second finger eased its way in. Kye was ready for him, eager for him, desperate for him.

The fingers were withdrawn and replaced with the head of Ian's cock. Ian penetrated him, the thud of his heart beating against Kye's back. "You okay?" Ian's voice was a hoarse whisper.

"Aye. Better than okay," Kye answered. Ian began to move, his rhythm matching Kye's and Cassidy's. Ian filled him, stretching him, consuming him, using him as a conduit to Cassidy with each sensual thrust. It was as if the three had literally become one. The vibrations of their movements penetrated Kye's muscles, pulsing in waves until they rattled his bones and made his heart thrum. The sensations were flowing in one unbroken circle between the three of them, any distinction superfluous.

Kye reached around Cassidy's body, finding the sweet, wet spread of her labia. He stroked her until she was breathless, her body shuddering with each thrust of Ian's cock into Kye, which in turned thrust him into her.

Ian gripped him from behind, slamming into him as he cried out. The dual climaxes sent Kye over the edge. The orgasm swept over him like surf sweeping up over sand and then falling back, and then sweeping up again and falling back. It was as if he were breaking up into a thousand tiny pieces, like bonfire sparks, tumbling up high in the air and then floating...floating down...

He found himself lying in a tangled heap with his two lovers. He must have lost consciousness for a second or two. Ian moved to his side and he in turn lifted himself from Cassidy, pulling her head to his shoulder.

Ian stripped the used condom from Kye's spent shaft and tossed it, along with his own, into the trash. Cassidy touched his face with soft fingertips, wiping away tears he hadn't known were there. Ian, again beside him, stroked his chest, whispering, "It's okay." A great sense of peace settled over him. He knew he didn't need to explain anything. They pressed in on either side and Kye closed his eyes, and in the darkness he could feel the whole world revolving. For the first time in his life, he was understood. The gypsy had finally found a home.

Chapter Fifteen

Together they maneuvered the mattress around the bend of the stairs. "Watch out for the photos," Cassidy cried, just as the corner of the mattress hit one of the framed photographs of Ian lying on the beach at sunset, staring pensively out at the ocean.

The wall along the stairs was lined with photographs Cassidy had taken over the years. Many of them were of Ian, or of the two of them together. Some were of his jewelry, the angle and focus of the pictures making them look like crystallized abstracts.

New photos had recently been added, including Kye and Ian, arm in arm beneath the old mimosa tree, and Kye on the porch strumming his guitar, his eyes closed, his face suffused with that special glow he got when he made music, and the three of them holding corn dogs and making silly faces in front of the big Ferris Wheel at the Texas State Fair, while waiting for the timer on the camera to go off.

After he'd returned from the Austin excursion, they'd settled back into their routines fairly rapidly, Kye picking up where he'd left off with the business end of things. Ian, along with Brenda, continued to work as fast and hard as he could to keep up with demand. Cassidy did the photography, the website and the direct marketing. Both Cassidy and Ian made a conscious effort not to rely so heavily on Kye as they had before he'd left.

They had been taking advantage of him, though that wasn't their intention. Instead of stepping up and learning what they needed to do to run their business, they'd gratefully shunted it off on him. When he took over various household duties, along with cooking the meals, they'd let him.

Cassidy had summed it up well. "Just because he's willing, doesn't make it right. He's not our man Friday, he's our partner and our friend. It's time we grew up, you and me."

It was Ian who made the decision to ask Brenda to join the business as a full-time artisan, though he'd discussed the financial aspects of it with Kye and Cassidy. Brenda had her own worktable alongside Ian's. He found he liked her company. She didn't talk much, nor did he, but it was nice to have someone who understood jewelry design to bounce his ideas off of.

Ian's old bed was queen-size, the mattress ancient. The new king-size bed had been Cassidy's idea. Kye still slipped away fairly often after they made love, returning to his single bed when he was ready to sleep. Cassidy thought maybe if they had a larger bed, he might be more inclined to stay.

Ian had laughed at this, teasing Cassidy that she'd still find a way to take up the entire bed, no matter how huge. She liked to spread out when she slept, all legs and arms. When she slept in his bed, many were the times he awoke to find himself on the edge of the mattress, completely devoid of blankets. Still, Kye had seemed pleased by the gesture, though he warned them he would still probably head off to his own bedroom from time to time.

For Kye's birthday, Ian had fashioned him a silver medallion he'd made by fitting three teardrop-shaped pieces so they were chasing one another round a circle. He'd copied the design from a Celtic sacred art book. To his delight, Kye was familiar with the design, which he said was called a triskele. Beaming with pleasure, Kye had added it at once to the chain he wore round his neck.

They had met Kye in the first week of April, when Houston was in the brief, vibrant flush of spring. Now as October loomed, the air was again touched with a cool tang, a hint of Southern autumn. Since Kye's return, they'd continued to work through the ups and downs of a new relationship, one more complex because there were three instead of just two.

Ian had continued to struggle, though for the most part silently, with issues of jealousy and insecurity. At first he'd been afraid the flush of renewed passion between Cassidy and himself would give over to the old tapes he'd played for so long when a relationship became intimate, but for the most part it didn't happen. He tried to be self-aware, recognizing when he was finding fault with one or both of them, that the issue was really his own fear, not anything they were doing.

It helped that Kye was there to keep him on his toes, and remind him by his very presence that Cassidy's affections were a gift, not a right, as were Kye's and, for that matter, his own.

Some mornings Ian would wake up, incredulous that his life seemed to be going so well. He was happier than he had ever been. Not only was their business thriving, but he found himself in the middle of the most amazing relationship he'd ever experienced. The sexual exploration between the three continued, and Ian now felt as confident making love to a man as to a woman.

He marveled sometimes that he was with these two amazing creatures, both so alike in some ways, both full of boundless energy, both ready to take any adventure by the horns and seize it. Ian was a counterbalance to their exuberance—taking a slower, more measured approach to things. But by the same token, they'd taught him to relax, to ease his grip and not try to control things so much.

Sometimes he still worried Kye would tire of them, or his wanderlust would take hold and they'd wake up one day to find a scrawled note of farewell, his duffel and guitar gone, his motorcycle no longer in the driveway. Still other times he wondered if Cassidy might stray—even the combined love of her two men no longer enough.

When he got these feelings, he reminded himself nothing lasts forever. That was part of what made life so precious. Any of them could leave at any time. The fact they each chose to stay, each chose to be a part of the others' lives for today, that was enough.

Kye had begun to explore Houston some on his own. He'd found several coffeehouses and open mics where his style of acoustic guitar was appreciated. From time to time he performed, always to great acclaim. He'd met a few other musicians and had begun to make his own network of friends. He'd invited them over a few times to the house for dinner, afterwards entertaining Cassidy and Ian with their music.

The three of them decided to throw a party to celebrate the burgeoning success of the jewelry business. They drew up a guest list, each contributing who they would like to invite. Included were friends and family, as well as clients, vendors and even Ian's old boss from the mall jewelry stores.

They had the event catered so they could focus on their guests. The party had been a great success. Brenda and Ian had worked overtime to prepare their latest offerings, beautifully displayed on their worktables in elegant glass showcases Kye had rented for the occasion. Ian was incredibly proud of Kye and Cassidy, moving so effortlessly through the crowd, ever the gracious host and hostess. He was proud of himself too.

Cassidy was radiant in a flowing silk gown of dark green, her auburn hair swept up in a French twist, her shoulders bare to show off the necklace he'd made especially for the event. It was a simple but arresting piece woven from multiple sterling silver strands, beaded with fresh water pearls and fluorite, the clear green gems mirroring her lovely eyes.

Kye and Ian had dressed up for the event as well, wearing elegant suits they'd rented for the occasion. Kye had joked that they cleaned up quite nicely when they put their minds to it. Ian had to agree. Kye was easily the most handsome man at the party, and received much attention.

Sometimes Ian could hardly believe how his life had fallen together. It wasn't long ago he was an employee being paid an hourly wage. With lots of hard work and good luck, together the three of them had turned a fledgling, struggling business into a viable, successful, if still very small enterprise. And at the rate they were going, who knew where they might be a year from now? Five years from now?

Kye was already talking about hiring more people and perhaps renting some warehouse space to set up a real office and workspace. It was hard to believe Cassidy's initial vision could turn into something so promising. He loved her all the more for her constant faith in him, and her gumption in getting him to take the leap of faith it required to get the business started.

Now that they were solidly back together, Ian decided to celebrate with something special. He'd been working on it a while, but the night before, determined to finish it, he had stayed up very late, hunkered over his worktable, not letting either of them see what he was working on. He told them it was a new design for the catalog, but it wasn't. No, what he was making would be one of a kind. Or rather, three of a kind.

He'd barely slept that night, slipping into bed beside his sleeping lovers sometime after two, and awakening a little after six o'clock to the rising sun. Grabbing a pair of pants and a knit shirt, he stole down the stairs, avoiding the two creaking ones so he wouldn't make any noise. He retrieved and opened the small jewelry box he'd hidden in one of the drawers beneath the worktable.

Three rings, identical except in size, were nestled against the black velvet that lined the box. He'd braided strands of yellow gold, rose gold and silver together in an open weave. He'd lined the inside of each ring with a smooth, thin wall of gold. What made the rings especially unique was that he'd created them from one long braided piece, from which he'd fashioned the three separate rings.

He smiled, pleased with the design, eager to show them to Kye and Cassidy. He was jittery with nervous anticipation. Cassidy wore several rings he'd given her over the years, but none of them had the import these did. Usually she saw something he was working on and asked him to make one for her. But this was different.

He wondered if Kye would wear his. He wore no rings and perhaps didn't like the feel of something on his finger. He could wear it on the chain around his neck, if it came to that. Or not at all. Ian told himself firmly it was a gift—a gift of the heart to the two people he loved best in the world. What they chose to do with the gift should be left entirely up to them.

He lifted one of the larger rings out of the box and slipped it on his left ring finger. It fit well. He himself had never worn a ring, but he liked the solid heft of it. He slipped it off and set it back beside the other two. He'd made Kye's ring slightly larger, having surreptitiously measured his finger one night while Kye was sleeping. He ran his finger over the three rings, vastly pleased, hoping they both would like them. Closing the box, he slid it into his pocket.

In the kitchen, he set about making coffee and hunting for the box of pancake mix. He'd let Cassidy and then Kye wait on him for so long, he barely knew where things were. True, he was the mainstay of the business—without him there was no Ian Tanner Designs, but that didn't mean he had to work on jewelry 24/7, and leave the running of the household entirely to the other two.

He found the eggs, the oil, the milk and the mix, and set about dumping the measured quantities into a mixing bowl. He turned on the griddle and found a package of bacon. When the coffee was brewed, he poured himself a cup, stirred in some cream, and sat for a moment at the table. As he sipped the hot coffee, he stared out the window, pleasantly content.

He heard the creaking stairs and turned just as Kye walked into the kitchen, his dark hair tousled, his face smudged with sleep. He was shirtless, though he wore long pants, the faded jeans he'd been wearing the first night Ian had met him, with the large hole in one knee. The medallion Ian had given him lay flat against his tan, smooth chest.

"Hey, early bird. What have you got going here?" Kye moved toward the cabinet and retrieved a coffee mug, pouring himself a cup and adding cream and sugar before joining Ian at the table.

"I made some pancake batter. I'm glad you're up. I've never actually made pancakes. You can give me a lesson."

"Well, you've come to the right guy." Kye grinned. "I think Cassidy's up too. I heard her stirring when I was washing up. I don't know why we're all up so early today. Especially you—we must have been asleep already by the time you rolled into bed."

"Yeah." Nearly bursting with his secret surprise, Ian tried to keep his face deadpan.

Apparently he didn't succeed, because Kye said, "To borrow an old phrase, you look like the cat that ate the canary. What're you hiding? Come on. Spill it."

"What?" Ian feigned innocence. He rose and began peeling strips of bacon from the slab, arranging them in a neat row on one side of the griddle.

Kye laughed. "Okay, have it your way. I'm sure you'll let us know in your own time."

Ian nodded, at once relieved and disappointed he hadn't

probed further. One little, "Oh, come on, you can tell me," and he would have spilled the beans. As it was, he let Kye give him a lesson in pancake making, from how long to mix your batter, to the proper temperature of the griddle, to the ideal time to flip the pancakes so they were cooked through but didn't burn. They had a nice stack of pancakes and a pile of crisp bacon beside it when Cassidy came into the kitchen.

"Yum, it smells good in here." She lifted her arms in a sensual stretch that for a moment distracted Ian from his pancake flipping. She was wearing one of his oversized T-shirts, her nipples poking provocatively through the fabric, her legs bare.

"Kye's teaching me to make pancakes."

"Good. Then you can teach me." She laughed. "I'll set the table."

Ian felt good, a part of something warm and cozy, as the three of them moved about the kitchen. Between them they set out the plates of food, butter, syrup and cream, the coffee mugs and the silverware. Cassidy poured herself some coffee and topped off theirs before sitting down to join them.

They ate in silence for a while—the pancakes had come out perfect, though Ian knew this was because Kye had hovered over him while he'd made them. But next time he'd do it alone. He kept glancing from one to the other as they ate, the jewelry box burning a hole in his pocket.

"Ian's got a secret." Kye winked at Cassidy.

"Does he?" She looked curiously at Ian, raising her eyebrows. "Ian can't keep a secret to save his life." She laughed, but her expression was kind and she laid her hand over his.

"It's true. I can't," he admitted. "But you'll just have to wait until we've finished breakfast. I think I can keep it that much longer." They finished their meal and put the dishes in the sink for later washing.

They stepped out onto the porch. The air was cool, a nice breeze moving the October air. Kye looked contentedly around the porch. "I think the weather's finally giving us a break. I'm going to get some paint for the porch and we can spiff this place up. We can paint the shutters to match."

"Do you ever miss Scotland? Do you miss your family and your home?" Cassidy couldn't imagine uprooting herself the way Kye had done.

"Aye, lass. Sometimes I do. I was thinking perhaps the three of us should take a trip to Scotland sometime soon. I'd like you to see where I come from. But this is my home now."

Deciding it was the perfect moment, Ian pulled the box from his pocket and flipped open the lid as they both leaned forward to see its contents. "I made them for us. For the three of us."

"Ian, they're beautiful," Cassidy breathed. "May I?" She plucked out the smallest of the three rings and turned it over and over in her hand.

"They're all three made from the same braid," Ian explained. "It symbolizes the fact we are three separate individuals who have chosen to weave our lives together." He knew he was blushing.

"It's a beautiful sentiment." Kye looked with admiration at the bands. "The work is exquisite. You should add a line of wedding rings to the business."

Afraid they would think he was overstepping, Ian felt compelled to say, "These aren't wedding rings. More like— friendship rings." Ian handed Kye's ring to him. "What I mean is, the two of you are my best friends in the world. I love you with all my heart. I didn't know it was possible to truly love two different people, but I understand now the heart has more than enough room.

"When I made these rings, it wasn't my intention to try to

stake a claim on either of you. I just wanted to create something—something unique shared between just us three. Something to remind us of what we have."

Kye took the remaining ring from the box and fixed his clear gray eyes on Ian. "Hold out your hand."

Ian did, and Kye slipped the ring onto Ian's left ring finger. As if they'd rehearsed it, he dropped his ring into Ian's hand. Ian handed it to Cassidy, who placed it on Kye's finger. She then dropped her ring into Ian's hand and held out her hand, her eyes filled with love that made Ian's heart swell near to bursting. He slid the ring onto her finger.

He removed his ring and held it up to the light. "There's one more thing. I put an inscription inside each ring. Actually it's in three parts. You read yours first, Kye. Then you, Cassidy. And then I'll read mine."

Kye pulled his ring from his finger. Peering inside, he read the curlicue script. "In dreams and..."

Cassidy removed her ring and read, "...in love, there are..."

And Ian finished, "...no impossibilities."

About the Author

Claire Thompson lives and writes in upstate New York. She has written over forty novels, many dealing with the romance of erotic submission, along with a newfound passion for m/m erotica.

To learn more about Claire Thompson, please visit www.clairethompson.net. Send an email to Claire at Claire@clairethompson.net and sign up for her newsletter to keep abreast of her latest work, events, happenings and contests.

Torn between the love he has...and the love he's always wanted.

Rough, Raw and Ready
© *2008 Lorelei James*
Rough Riders Series, Book 5

Chassie West Glanzer hasn't been a stranger to drama and tragedy. A year of wedded bliss to sexy-as-sin cowboy Trevor Glanzer has brought her the happiness and contentment she never thought she'd find, and mellowed Trevor's rodeo wanderlust. Then Trevor's old roping partner ambles up the driveway—and Chassie's life changes drastically.

Trevor never expected to see Edgard Mancuso again, after it became clear he couldn't be the man Edgard needed. Now Edgard is back from Brazil to sort out their tangled past, and Trevor is plagued with feelings he thought he'd buried over three years ago. Although Trevor is hat-over-bootheels in love with his sweet, feisty wife, the sense his life is missing a piece has always gnawed at him.

Chassie's shock that Edgard and Trevor were once lovers turns to fear of losing her husband. Or worse, fear that Trevor will stay with her only out of a sense of duty. Yet as the three of them spend time together, the sins of the past blur and fade, leaving raw emotion—and unbridled passion.

Passion that could heal...or cause irreparable damage to their future.

Warning: this book contains unbelievably explicit sex, including multiple cowboy/cowgirl/cowboy ménage scenes, juicy, hot, male on male action, a bucketful of politically incorrect situations and true Western ideology.

Available now in ebook and print from Samhain Publishing.

Enjoy the following excerpt from Rough, Raw and Ready...

By the time Trevor finished scrubbing the machine oil from his hands, Chassie and Edgard had returned to the kitchen.

Chassie said, "Who wants coffee?"

"Sounds great, Chass."

"There's cookies, unless Trev ate them all. The man has a serious sweet tooth."

"Then I oughta munch on you, darlin', since you're so durn sweet." Trevor nibbled the side of her jaw and Chassie squealed. He reached above her head for the coffee cups on the pegs.

Trevor turned and saw Edgard staring at them. Not with jealousy, but with longing. Simple affectionate moments had been rare between them and Trevor remembered it was one of the things Edgard had needed that Trevor hadn't been able to offer him. Why did he feel just as guilty about that shortcoming now as he had back then?

Chassie poured the coffee. Trevor automatically grabbed the milk jug from the fridge and set it next to Edgard. He snagged a spoon from the dish rack, passing it and the sugar canister to Edgard, ignoring Chassie's questioning stare.

Didn't mean a damn thing he remembered exactly how Edgard liked his coffee. Not a damn thing.

"So, Edgard, what are you doin' in our neck of the woods?"

"Reliving some old memories. I drove past my grandparents' place yesterday. With the shabby way it's looking I'm wishing I would've bought it when I had the chance." He smiled wryly. "I'm kicking myself for letting another thing slip through my fingers."

"Grandparents?" Chassie repeated, not noticing Trevor's rigid posture after Edgard's comment. "You from around here?"

"Yes. And no." Edgard relayed the story about his mother.

Getting pregnant as a foreign exchange student, giving birth to Edgard before his biological father, a young cowboy, died in an accident. She'd returned home to Brazil and married Edgard's stepfather.

"Whoa. That's kind of soap-operaish, isn't it?"

"Mmm-hmm." Edgard blew across his coffee. "But it does make me an American citizen so I can come and go as I please in the good ol' U.S. of A."

Trevor listened as Chassie asked a million questions about Edgard's life and Brazil. They finished off the pot of coffee and the time passed pleasantly. He even managed to meet Edgard's gaze a couple of times.

The phone rang and Chassie excused herself to answer it.

Silence hung between them as heavy as snow clouds in a winter sky.

Eventually, Edgard said, "She doesn't know anything about me. Not even that we were roping partners. Not that we were…" He looked at Trevor expectantly.

"No." Trevor quickly glanced at the living room where Chassie was chattering away. "You surprised?"

"Maybe that she isn't aware of our official association as roping partners. There was no shame in that. We were damn good together, Trev."

The word *shame* echoed like a slap. As good as they were together, it'd never been enough, in an official capacity or behind closed doors. "What are you really doin' here?"

Edgard didn't answer right away. "I don't know. Feeling restless. Had the urge to travel."

"Wyoming ain't exactly an exotic port of call."

"You think I don't realize that? You think I wouldn't rather be someplace else? But something…" Edgard lowered his voice. "Ah, fuck it."

"What?"

"Want the truth? Or would you rather I lie?"

"The truth."

"Truth between us? That's refreshing." Edgard's gaze trapped his. "I'm here because of you."

Trevor's heart alternately stopped and soared, even when his answer was an indiscernible growl. "For Christsake, Ed. What the hell am I supposed to say to that? With my wife in the next room?"

"You're making a big deal out of this. She thinks we're friends, which ain't a lie. We were partners before we were..." Edgard gestured distractedly. "If she gets the wrong idea, it won't be from me."

"Maybe *I'm* gettin' the wrong idea. The last thing you said to me when you fuckin' *left* me was that you weren't ever comin' back. And you made it goddamn clear you didn't want to be my friend. So why are you here?"

Pause. He traced the rim of his coffee cup with a shaking fingertip. "I heard about you gettin' married."

"That happened over a year ago and you came all the way from Brazil to congratulate me in person? Now?"

"No." Edgard didn't seem to know what to do with his hands. He raked his fingers through his hair. His voice was barely audible. "Will it piss you off if I admit I was curious about whether you're really happy, *meu amore?*"

My love. My ass. Trevor snapped, "Yes."

"Yes, you're pissed off? Or yes, you're happy?"

"Both."

"Then this is gonna piss you off even more."

"What?"

"Years and miles haven't changed anything between us and you goddamn well know it."

Trevor looked up; Edgard's golden eyes were laser beams slicing him open. "It don't matter. If you can't be my *friend* while you're in my house, walk out the fuckin' door. I will not allow either one of us to hurt my wife. Got it?"

"Yeah."

"Good. And I'm done talkin' about this shit so don't bring it up again. Ever."

Chassie bounded back into the kitchen. If she sensed the tension she didn't remark on it. "My coffee break is over. Gotta get back to the grind. What're you guys gonna do?"

Trevor gathered the cups and dumped them in the sink. "I'll help you finish up outside."

"No, that's okay. You stay and catch up with Edgard."

"Darlin', it ain't every day I offer to let you boss me around," Trevor pointed out with a teasing smile.

Edgard stood. "If it's all right, I might stretch out. I'm bushed. Been a long morning and a long walk this afternoon."

Trevor stared at him. Edgard had walked the twenty-five miles from town? In the cold?

"If you're hungry later, help yourself to whatever you can find. I already showed you where the towels and stuff are in the bathroom so make yourself at home."

"Thank you, Chassie, you are very kind." Edgard headed for the stairs.

When he was gone, Chassie hooked her fingers in Trevor's belt loop. "Come on, you're my slave for the next couple hours."

"Mmm. I like the sound of that." He lowered his head, teasing her lips before plunging his tongue inside her sweet, warm mouth. Kissing her until her heart raced beneath his palm and her body swayed closer. Trevor pulled back so they were a breath apart. "But I get my shot at bein' the master to your slave later, right?"

Her soft moan smacked of sexual need and instantly stiffened his cock. "No ropes this time."

"That ain't no fun."

"Neither is disinfecting the birthing equipment in the barn."

Trevor groaned. "*That's* what we're doin' today?"

"Yep. Has to be done when it's not sub-zero outside and you volunteered, bucko."

"Lead on, master."

She grinned. After she turned around, Trevor whacked her on the ass hard enough to elicit a yelp and she ran away from him, laughing.

Damn. He loved being married to this woman. He'd be wise to remember that.

Discover eBooks!

THE FASTEST WAY TO GET THE HOTTEST NAMES

Get your favorite authors on your favorite reader, long before they're
out in print! Ebooks from Samhain go wherever you go, and work with
whatever you carry—Palm, PDF, Mobi, and more.

LaVergne, TN USA
25 October 2009
161971LV00004B/1/P